I0691401

AN ICONOCLAST THRILLER: BOOK 1

RAVENS COVE

THE SUPERNATURAL BATTLE
FOR A SMALL ALASKA TOWN

By Mary Ann Poll

America's Lady of Supernatural Thrillers
Author Masterminds Charter Member

PUBLICATION
CONSULTANTS
We Believe In The Power Of Authors

PO Box 221974 Anchorage, Alaska 99522-1974
books@publicationconsultants.com, www.publicationconsultants.com

ISBN Number: 978-1-59433-864-9
eBook ISBN Number: 978-1-59433-865-6

Library of Congress Catalog Card Number: 2019934847

Copyright 2019 Mary Ann Poll
—Second Edition—

All rights reserved, including the right of
reproduction in any form, or by any mechanical
or electronic means including photocopying or
recording, or by any information storage or
retrieval system, in whole or in part in any
form, and in any case not without the
written permission of the author and publisher.

Manufactured in the United States of America

Dedication

To John, Daniel, and Rhonda. Without your love, patience, and support *Ravens Cove* would still be just an idea.

ACKNOWLEDGEMENTS

I am grateful to have this opportunity to offer my thanks to those that have helped make this book possible.

Dr. Dwayne Poll – if you had not been willing to read and edit the roughest of all the drafts, I would not have found the courage to 'go the distance.'

My friend and mentor, Frank Redman. Your advice and guidance has improved *Ravens Cove* and made it an amazing debut novel.

My friends at Kyllonen's RV Park (Susan Kyllonen and Ralph and Kathy Ahart) in Anchor Point, Alaska—You gave me a retreat in a glorious natural setting when I needed it most. You inspired the town of Ravens Cove.

Wikipedia, that wonderful internet encyclopedia, that gave me a crash course on Captain Cook and his voyage to Alaska.

Cornwall Model Boats, another internet resource, for posting a wonderful replica of the *HMS Resolution*.

Last, but not least as they say, to all my good friends who stuck by me even when they didn't hear from me for weeks or months. You bless my life.

CONTENTS

Prologue   The Legend Wakes 9

Chapter 1   A Corpse on Corpse Mound. 21

Chapter 2   A Man On a Mission. 30

Chapter 3   Visions and Disbelief 36

Chapter 4   Dark and Light. 40

Chapter 5   The Ultimatum 45

Chapter 6   A Secret Life 47

Chapter 7   No Is Not an Option. 50

Chapter 8   Day's End 55

Chapter 9   The Darkness Grows 63

Chapter 10   Grievous Memories 66

Chapter 11   A Tenuous Truce. 69

Chapter 12   A Suspect Surfaces 75

Chapter 13   An Angel Speaks. 78

Chapter 14   A Better Suspect 80

Chapter 15   Secrets. 87

Chapter 16   Truths 92

Chapter 17   The Legend Revealed........................102

Chapter 18   Black Cat.................................114

Chapter 19   Prayers and Plots.........................117

Chapter 20   Heralds of Destruction.....................124

Chapter 21   Unwelcome Visitors.......................126

Chapter 22   The Attack...............................135

Chapter 23   A Secret Weapon.........................144

Chapter 24   Out of the Ashes.........................149

Chapter 25   Legend or Truth.........................152

Chapter 26   A Woman Scorned.......................156

Chapter 27   Safety in Numbers........................162

Chapter 28   Jo's Strange Story........................167

Chapter 29   Guarding the Ravine......................170

Chapter 30   Another Lost Soul........................172

Chapter 31   The Trap................................175

Chapter 32   Into the Ravine..........................179

Chapter 33   Against All Odds.........................182

Epilogue   The Legend Sleeps........................189

THE LEGEND WAKES

May, 1778

Seaman Sweeney Giles lay stock-still in a thicket beneath a stand of leaf-bare birch and willow trees. The full white moon silhouetted the HMS *Resolution* and HMS *Discovery*, spotlighting their open masts.

Even at this distance, he heard the familiar sound of the ships' sails snapping and the halyards thumping in an increasing wind. The *Resolution* bobbed and pulled on its restraining anchors, mimicked seconds later by its consort ship, ready to be gone from this dark place.

"They's be looking fo' me fo' sure," he muttered to the twisted stump of a long-dead, rotten-smelling birch. Its offspring, along with several anemic spruces, surrounded the stump.

"Mr. Giles," a far-away voice called.

Holding his breath, Sweeney, or Tooth, as the rest of the crew so nastily nicknamed him because of his large, protruding, white tooth, pushed up on both hands to locate the author of the voice.

"He's close. I'm havin' to move soon."

Sweeney inched up to the stand of birch and spruce trees, peeking through late-autumn branches. Branches which moments ago danced in the calm breeze, snapped backward and slapped him as the wind increased.

"They'd want to be settin' sail soon."

"Mr. Giles," a different crew member's voice echoed through the wraithlike moonlight.

Boots cracked the dry leaves and grasses no more than thirty feet to his right.

Sweeney shoved, hands slipping as dry leaves gave way to slimy wet ones. He landed nose first in the decay. He jerked his head up and listened, fearing he would be discovered.

No footsteps.

Sweeney peeked through the tree branches. Faceless silhouettes dotted the landscape, black against the silver spotlight of the moon. The countryside to his right and left consisted of dead grass and marsh, which did well to hide his tracks when he ran to the thicket.

"But not now," he whispered.

His shipmates were so close now, the *crack* of the dead grass would only serve to reveal his whereabouts. He jerked his head to the rear. An opaque mist shrouded the landscape behind him.

"I know not where I are goin', but I ain't gettin' caught. I are free at last!"

Sweeney's past flooded his mind. At 17, he knew far too much about the fear of pain and death. Guy Tillmooth saw to it. Every day of Sweeney's young life testified to it. But the torture ended with the death of the old man.

Sweeney smiled when he remembered the day his father decided to lash him again—this time with the mare's halter.

Sweeney didn't remember grabbing the pitchfork hanging inside the broken-down shanty of a barn. He did recall small shafts of light illuminating Guy Tillmooth's hulk and the old man's face—sweat running into the wild, excited red eyes.

All the beatings, all the venomous words spewed at him, all the preaching and drinking and beatings his mum took in his place, crashed through his brain in a vengeful wave.

He lunged.

The pitchfork caught Guy Tillmooth in his gut, throwing the elder Tillmooth backward into the hay, dirt, and filthy wreckage of the barn.

"Glory, killin' him were good," Tooth muttered, remembering the satisfying pop of flesh giving way to the fork. His smile widened when he thought of the smell of blood mixed with dirt, sweat and hay.

Winded and shaken, he leaned on the wall, a hand still on the pitchfork in his father's belly.

Recovering from the initial shock, Guy Tillmooth howled, stood, and made an unsuccessful attempt to pull the tool out of his body.

"But I are a *vigrus* one, Mum always said." In actuality, the fear of his father's rage renewed the younger Sweeney's strength.

He loosed the fork and drove it in again.

"His bones cracked and the old screw gurgled a yell and dropped to his knees. He weren't able to speak, so 'is eyes pleaded with me to spare him."

Tooth's sneer widened, the white dagger shining from his lips. "Old fool! He ne'er showed me any niceties. Turn about's fair play!

"So I done him off, then. I kicked the old man's head so hard it cracked."

Guy Sweeney fell with a satisfying *thud.*

Tooth sprung off the ground and came down, both feet, on his father's head.

"It popped like a melon," Sweeney whispered, reveling in the memory.

All too soon to his taste, the cold reality of survival replaced the headiness of vengeance. Sweeney ran to the old, run-down shack of a house, grabbed a butcher knife, a shirt, a meat pie and never looked back.

When night fell, a shaking, tired and disheveled Sweeney slept in the woods. Before sunrise, he bolted upright, hands to his throat and gasping for breath.

The dream had been too real for his liking—he could still feel the noose tight on his wiry neck.

"Think, Tillmooth, think." Tooth banged his forehead with the palm of his hand, then stopped.

"I knows what I must do!"

Sweeney Tillmooth had none too much for brains but made up for it in a shrewdness born from the desire to live.

He found his salvation in a Mr. John Giles at the local pub on the docks.

"Couldn't help but overhear," Tooth said.

Giles turned his head left to scrutinize this stranger. Repulsed by the razor-toothed grin, he swung around on the bar stool and concentrated on the dark ale in front of him.

The disgust in the man's eyes did not escape Tooth. The rage rose. He took a deep breath to relax.

"None to 'appy 'bout sailing, huh?"

"None. No way 'round though," Giles growled. "Can't find no other job. The family 'as to eat."

"Bad way. Leavin' those ya love for so long."

Giles grunted. He looked at Tooth again. "What 'appened to yer teeth?"

"Bad luck. Just bad luck."

Giles scrutinized Tooth's mouth. "Mus' be hard."

The rage simmered to a boiling point. Sweeney hated pity more than he hated a beating.

"'Deed." He choked out.

They sat in silence, each in his own thoughts.

Sweeney glanced sideways at Giles. "Buy you another?"

Giles lit up like a candle. "'Deed."

Drunk in no time, Giles leaned unsteadily on Tooth, and walked into the night with a newborn murderer, hungry for his next victim. Late and quiet they rounded a building to "relieve his self," as Tooth explained.

Giles turned his back to give Tooth some privacy.

Now's my chance.

In one fluid movement, Tooth removed the knife and slit Giles' neck. He watched Giles drop to the ground in a puddle of blood, thrashing and gurgling in the final throes of death. He felt the power of new life fill him as he watched Giles, eyes glazed in death, become just a bag of flesh.

"Thanks much, Johnny boy." Sweeney smiled, black gums absorbing moonlight as shadows absorb light.

Tooth became John Sweeney Giles and joined the *Resolution* crew. The crew called him Sweeney when they weren't demeaning him as Tooth.

He became a sailor under Captain Cook to run as far as he could from the memory of the drunk, horrid man who fathered him.

Irony raised its ugly head when he again faced a similarly cruel man in Captain Cook.

The Captain seemed fine enough in the beginning but became a raging lunatic during Sweeney's first voyage. Sweeney cleaned the decks so many times a day his hands blistered and bled.

No one ate or drank until Cook's specifications were satisfied. When they were allowed to eat, the crew was forced to consume walrus meat, which Sweeney could barely choke down and which caused half the crew to vomit.

To make matters worse, Cook's obsession with the Northwest Passage endangered everyone. He would not rest. Cook sent the crew into storming seas in small boats at all hours of the day or night, anytime his crazed mind filled with fear of *something* unknown.

"Mr. Giles! Mr. Giles, where are you?"

The voices brought Sweeney back to the present. *They's close. I's gotta move— and fast. I's can't let 'em catch me, I be hanged fo' sure!*

Using the palms of his hands, Sweeney pushed and slithered backward in the ravine, putting distance between him and the voices.

Pain seared through Sweeney's left calf. He stifled the shocked scream. Any noise would reveal his location.

He rolled to his side and searched the darkness.

A blood-red arrowhead protruded from his left knee. The deep cut ran from right below the knee to his ankle. Torn pants gave way to a view of torn skin and muscle. He yanked the arrowhead from his leg.

Sweeney examined the cause of his pain in the pale moonlight.

"Ye ain't red at all. Ye be glowing!" he whispered.

Tooth examined the arrowhead more closely. "What be you? Are you black magic like the fools at 'ome are feared of? If you be, I ain't afeared."

He stared into the rock. *It be beatin' like a heart!* he thought.

With each throb, it emitted a brilliant violet light pulling Sweeney into another world. Visions filled his head. He saw himself king of this barren land, all bowing to him.

"No one here to bow," he said to the stone.

Sweeney shook his head and remembered the wound. He looked at his leg, gauging how much of his shirt he'd need for the bandage.

Only a purple scar from calf to knee, the color of the pulsing stone, remained.

"I'm gettin' crazy as Cook," he muttered.

For the first time in a long time, Sweeney felt terror, an emotion he purposely buried in his subconscious long ago.

"Foolishness," he muttered.

He heard the footsteps of the sailors even closer.

He scurried backward again; the ground beneath him collapsed. Sweeney found himself in an uncontrollable fall.

I be dead fo' sure, he thought. He tensed, squinted his eyes shut and waited for the end.

He stopped with a loud *whack.*

A misshapen hag of a tree stood between him and the precipice. Its branches vibrated from the impact of Sweeney's weight.

"Thank ye!"

The trunk creaked and bent forward, its bony, dark fingers reaching for him.

"Crazier by the minute," he lamented.

Sweeney checked for injuries. He recoiled in pain when he tested his right foot. The left, however, possessed unexplained strength and stabilized him on the sloping path.

He heard his shipmates still calling his name. Relief flooded him when he realized they were much farther away. To his surprise, the chasm hid him from the rest of the world. In fact, the silence in the ravine reminded him of midnight in the woods close to his home in England.

"I have no 'ome," he said. "Sweeney Tillmooth is no more."

Tooth made a careful turn, so as not to slip again, and looked into the blackness. His right hand pulsed. He unclenched his fingers and smiled to know he still held his newfound treasure.

Dark purple, black, and red swirled through the stone.

"How can this be?" he asked.

The rock's swirling colors hypnotized Sweeney. He again saw himself the king of this land; the one who they—whoever they were—were waiting for.

He saw his subjects bowing before him, bringing him gifts, bringing him *blood* gifts, *human* blood gifts. Sweeney's mouth widened into a sinister grin. A sneer made even more menacing by the weapon of a front tooth protruding from his upper lip.

He returned from this glorious vision to see a ball of pulsing light, reflecting the stone's colors, floating toward him.

Sweeney swirled around, using his left foot to scuttle up the ravine.

He slid back to the hag tree, an invisible magnet pulling him farther into the black maw of the gorge.

Trapped, he thought.

The orb bobbed up and down and in a slow, steady pace, advanced toward him, just as his mum said it did when you, "Is gettin' ready to die."

"No! The will-o-the-wisp tale is the rambles of a crazy woman, livin' too long with the devil-man Guy Tillmooth."

He pushed with his foot again and slid back to the hag tree. He fell, spread-eagle on the ground, his good foot against the trunk.

The orb came closer; Sweeney gazed deep into its light. His brow furrowed, then he relaxed. *The orb is my friend.*

Counting his beloved treasure, he made two friends today. *More than my whole life.*

This one confirmed he *would* be king and the One. He saw it reflected in the purple, red, and black pulsing inside the dirty yellow light. It stopped advancing and hovered over his chest. Its pulse and his were in rhythm.

"Sweeney Tillmooth, you will have all the power, all the respect you have always known you deserved. You will prey on the weak, destroy the ones who think they are powerful and consume them to make *you* even *stronger*." The being dripped yellow light into Sweeney's welcoming heart.

Tooth felt cold; all emotion drained from him.

The creature pulled its members out of his heart, made a two-fingered hand and pointed him deeper into the ravine. The jaundiced digits shot ochre light out into the chasm of darkness.

Below him, copies of the hag tree lined the path.

"I see my new home!"

Tooth's new subjects smiled in welcome, exposing sharp, white teeth and flashing red eyes.

He took a timid step forward, stopped and looked over his shoulder.

A small voice warned him away, nagging at him to return to his ship and go home.

"This *is* my 'ome; my futurity," he announced. "Who cares if they hear? I's safe now and could kill them all. Come for me, my mates."

Tooth beckoned with his finger, realizing it oozed the yellow bony light. He looked at his chest and recognized it no longer. It seeped yellow, black, and red, which made its way down his stomach, splitting and flowing down both legs. He watched the slimy ebony substance absorb the mesmerizing colors.

A twig snapped.

Tooth spun around and faced the head of the path. He surveyed the darkness. As clear as if it were day, he saw a snow rabbit, turning white for the coming winter.

"A sacrifice!" He seized and devoured it. The satisfying crunch of the bones and the juicy organs refreshed him. To his delight, he also tasted its fear. The terror empowered his soul.

"Yes, come, my mates. Ye'd taste good 'ndeed."

He started forward.

A brilliant blue light filled the darkness.

One foot poised to step through the arch, he stopped in midstride. Tooth squinted, then covered his eyes with both hands as the glow intensified.

The fire-blue light shot toward him.

Tooth fell to his knees.

"Sweeney Tillmooth do not go in."

The voice rushed toward him, a cascade of thunder and music flowing over him.

"You can still return to the living."

"Who are ye. *What* are ye?" Tooth croaked.

The gooey yellow membrane retreated to a few feet behind him.

"Tell it to go! He is not your friend," it hissed.

"I am Raphael, a messenger of the One who was, Who is, and Who is to come! Turn back, Sweeney Tillmooth."

Sweeney considered.

The small voice inside of him spoke again. *Sweeney, abide me, turn back,* it pleaded.

Sweeney danced, his weight on one foot then the other.

"I needs to think." He smacked his forehead with the butt of his hand in a one-two rhythm.

The yellow being shot pencil-thin tendrils into his brain and whispered, "Remember the constant beatings, the verbal and physical lashings. On you, your mum. All because you were given a drunkard as a father. "The *One* this angel speaks of made you Guy Tillmooth's son.

"*I* am Gambogian," the voice hissed through the membrane. "I will give you this land. I will give you *power.*"

The voice bounced through Sweeney's mind, injecting malevolent thoughts and visions.

Hatred rose in Sweeney like a submerged buoy rising to the top of the ocean.

"Where were this One when I were a boy? Where?" he screamed.

Gambogian pulsed closer to Sweeney, caressing his hatred.

Raphael spoke. "Always there, Sweeney, watching, loving. He does not will any should perish! You can still choose life."

Tooth considered. *I murdered my own father, another sailor and a rabbit, if I's can murder a rabbit.*

"You can rule this land or hang. Choose!" Gambogian snarled.

"I will not hang! Out of the way," Tooth said, trembling, "I said out of the way! I have chosen to never be abandoned by your God again!"

"As you wish."

The blue-white light dulled, and Raphael shot to the sky like a rising star in the night.

"Good, Sweeney," Gambogian said, "excellent. Now, go through the doorway to your new kingdom and claim the power which awaits!"

Sweeney looked toward the trees arching above the entrance to the flat bottom of the ravine. His hands sweated, heart raced. He hesitated.

"Go through, now!"

"My own kingdom," Sweeney declared and pulled himself up to his full height and stepped forward.

The darkness absorbed all light. Sweeney felt something in front of him. Sulfur and decay penetrated his nostrils.

The presence growled, then laughed.

"Who's th-th-there?"

"I always answer a dying request," it snarled. "My name is Iconoclast, and I am your destiny."

Sweeney heard the moist sounds of lips being licked.

Sweeney turned and ran, but the darkness engulfed him. Somehow, he made it to the doorway, clawing at the hag trees surrounding it.

He screamed for help, but his shrieks were silent in the evil one's lair. He continued to yell as he felt the first bite sear through the scar now pulsing an iridescent purple. His silenced screams continued for hours.

When Iconoclast finished eating Sweeney's soul, flesh, and mind, he belched in satisfaction.

The arrowhead lay on the ground.

Iconoclast scooped it up. His fingers curled around it.

"Good, good Pet," Iconoclast said.

The stone throbbed black to black and purred.

Gambogian joined Iconoclast and Pet. "Pathetic humans! Give one an empty promise, and we easily take a life."

They laughed as Iconoclast tossed the shell of Sweeney Tillmooth to the top of the ravine. It fell with a sloshy thud.

Sweeney's shipmates found his remains. They ran. They ran as if pursued by the hounds of Hades.

None of the crew heard the growls and sniggers echoing around them when they sprinted back to the boats along the shore. And if asked, the crew would say they never found Sweeney. He just vanished.

Yet all who saw him would be forever haunted by the hideous image of Sweeney's body seeping jaundiced yellow from his pores, black and purple goo from the eyes, and a skeleton's smile on his face—and missing his prized, sharpened tooth.

Sweeney's final resting place never grew a living thing. The earth lay tarred and reeked a fetid odor as a warning for all who came near. It became known as Raven's Ravine—The Haunted Place.

CHAPTER 1

A CORPSE ON CORPSE MOUND

Kat gripped a large soup cup of coffee, warming her hands as she watched the late-October sunrise from her porch. The day came up cold and blue, the crystalline sky announcing the dawn. Little by little, she turned to the west, the morning clouds of peach tinged in grey leaving her sight. A view of Cook Inlet replaced the eastern scene.

"Good morning, Tikahtnu," she breathed her favorite name for the Cook Inlet. "Thank you, Tikahtnu, for sustaining the Denali Indians and the white settlers who joined them here."

A mist rose over Tikahtnu, cold meeting the heat of a new morning sun. The mountains across the water were purple from the mist but today the volcano stood in its full glory—high, clothed in wisps of light pink clouds.

A gust of cold wind shattered the morning warmth. Kat shivered and tightened her grip on the coffee cup. She inhaled the saltwater-laced air, invigorated by the scent. With one last look at the volcano, she turned, opened the heavy wood front door of her cabin and walked through.

A black blur rose up from behind the red footstool at the end of her couch and pounced.

"Ouch, for heaven's sake, BC, knock it off."

Kat jumped back, annoyed, the tranquility of her morning broken by her mischievous, self-absorbed feline.

"I should have left you for dead."

Tail in air, signaling his mission a complete success, BC sauntered to the small bedroom off the living room and combined kitchen area which made up Kat's home.

Focus, Kat, focus. She turned to her old blond desk, running a finger along one of its many scratches and nicks, avoiding the stress for a moment longer.

"You need to decide what to do with your life, girl. Enough of living in this small town, writing poems, doing some art, making trinkets for the tourists, and hoping to have enough to live on until the beginning of the next funnel-head invasion."

Resolving to the task, she thumped her coffee cup down on the desk, splashing a small amount onto a poem in progress. Facing the monitor, she clicked the Internet link and began perusing the many advertisements for online colleges.

A loud rap at the front door brought her out of the Internet fog saturating her brain.

Another knock, more impatient this time, followed by a familiar voice, shouting, "Open up, KittyKat. I know you're in there. Come out, come out wherever you are!"

Kat pushed back from her desk, bumping her knee on the corner and nearly spilling her coffee. "Ugh!"

She opened the door to Wendy Hareling, her lifelong friend.

"Oh, look, it's my annoying lifelong friend!"

Wendy breezed past Kat into the cabin.

Kat glared at her while bowing and extending her arm. "Do come in."

Wendy responded with a bow of mock courtesy. "Don't mind if I do, Ms. KittyKat."

"What brings you here so early in the morning?"

"News! Real news!

"There's been a murder, Kat—a murder in Ravens Cove!" Wendy started yanking on Kat's arm. "Come on, let's go see!"

Kat resisted, planting both feet on the worn wood-plank flooring. Dread replaced the irritation she felt moments before. "Who is it?"

"Don't know; no one knows him."

Kat relaxed, guilt niggling her gut because she felt relief instead of concern for this stranger.

"Sheriff Andersen is in a real dither. This sleepy old town is jumping for once. Let's go!"

"Your concern for others is not one of your strong suits. In fact, you should have moved to Hollywood, Winsome. Your drama would be appreciated in Tinsel Town."

The familiar nickname mocked Wendy as it had for years. Wendy stuck her tongue out at Kat, crossed her arms and plopped on the couch.

"See what I mean? Your drama is wasted in Ravens Cove."

Wendy rose. "I will forget you said that."

BC, in the act of settling into a warm Wendy lap, tumbled to the floor, feet first of course. He sat, tail swishing from side to side, considering his plan of attack.

Seeing this, Kat said, "Yes, I believe we should go before you can't walk."

Wendy looked at BC and swung her leg to the left right before he pounced.

"Missed, you mean, black thing! Why do you keep this cat, Kat?" Wendy smiled at the double meaning.

"He's my protector. Can't you see?"

BC walked over to Kat and twined through her legs, rubbing black hair all over her clean beige pants. She bent and made several swipes at the hairs, imbedding them farther with each attempt.

Wendy sniggered. "Well, maybe if you named him, he'd be a happier animal. BC for black cat. How original is Black Cat anyway?"

"Let's go, Winsome. Enough criticism of my name choices and your theories of how names affect animal behavior. Sheesh!"

Kat grabbed her coat and headed for the door, which made a satisfying *click* as she closed it.

The clouds hanging over the Cook Inlet earlier were gone. Kat and Wendy walked out into the late-October sun burning overhead.

The gravel driveway crunched under their shoes as they strode toward the dirt road leading to Kat's home. Ravens, jet-black against the blue sky, played in the wind, swooping toward earth then reversing the maneuver and streaking upward to meet a friend and dive together in a spontaneous air show.

Main Street buzzed with activity.

"You weren't wrong about the gossip."

"When have I ever been wrong about gossip, Kat?"

Kat tapped her lips with a finger. "I can't remember when you've ever been wrong about gossip."

"It is my job, you know."

"A great mission, Wendy. To know almost everything going on in this small Southcentral Alaskan town."

"Someone's gotta do it!"

"Oh, that can't be good." Kat pointed to a pair of identical twins.

Jonathan and Joseph Northan, the 20-something delinquents of Ravens Cove, stood by Jo's Bakery, heads together, in an animated conversation.

"Afraid they'll get blamed!"

"Well, don't know what's going on, but they *should* worry after all the trouble they've caused."

"They said he had no skin! They said his eyes were dribbling black and purple stuff!"

"Who's 'they' Ms. Conner?" Kat asked the town's second most dramatic person. *It is obvious this librarian shouldn't have access to the horror section.*

Anita Conner lifted her head, speaking down to Kat. "Those who saw the corpse!" She sniffed—closer to a huff—and turned from Kat.

"All righty then," Kat glanced at Wendy and rolled her eyes.

"I told you so."

Sheriff Bart Andersen—whose formal title was Police Chief— lifted his head at the sound of Kat's voice. He excused himself from the conversation with Mayor Orthell, and beelined it for Kat.

"We aren't finished here, Chief," Mayor Orthell said to Bart's back.

"Sheriff, sir."

"Your official title is Police Chief! There are no sheriffs in Alaska."

"There's one now," Bart answered.

Mayor Orthell shook his head and walked toward City Hall.

"Why do you antagonize Mayor Orthell that way?" Kat asked Bart. "It'll get you in trouble someday."

"Police Chief is too formal. People respond better to Sheriff."

"If you say so."

"I do. Anyway, glad you're here. We need to get to the office, pronto. Phones are going to be ringing off the hook."

Kat, secretary for the good sheriff of Ravens Cove when the need arose, looked up at Bart. Deep lines creased his rugged, youthful face. Uneasiness rose up from her gut to her heart.

Bart hooked Kat's elbow in his hand and guided her into the three-room storefront on Main Street—the town's police station. The rarely occupied jail cell in the back made it—but barely— four rooms.

Turning to face her, he took her shoulders in a gentle but firm grip. "I want you to start locking your door at night. Whoever committed this murder is a real psycho."

Kat stared, eyes wide, into Bart's sincere brown ones.

He responded to her silent question, "Amos Thralling found a body at the top of Ravens Ravine this morning. The way the victim met his demise, well, I've never seen anything like it." Bart paused, shook his head. "Not even in the classes I've attended on crime scene investigation. This one is going to take some major police work just to find the murder weapon, or weapons. And you know what's almost as bad?"

"No."

"We're going to have to send the body to Anchorage to find out what killed him. Then all those outsiders from the Alaska State Troopers, and maybe the FBI, are going to find out. They'll swoop in to take the glory and muddle up my investigation in the process."

"Okay . . ." Kat answered.

"Anyway, here are my first notes for the report." He shoved them into Kat's hand. "Read them and see what you think.

"I know you like to do research on your ole computer. Maybe if you get the time, you could take a look. You might come across something helpful in your technology travels."

Kat eased into the desk chair and read, "Amos Thralling said he took his usual route to the Cook Inlet when he saw what he thought to be a garbage drop. When he approached, he became aware of a stink he attributed to said garbage. The smell of decaying flesh made him throw up. He got close enough to see the remains of a man. Upon this discovery, Mr. Thralling 'ran like his pants were on fire,' his words, directly to the sheriff's office. Mr. Thralling accompanied me to said location of the body.

"Upon arrival, I observed decayed flesh, yellow in color, seeping into the ground. The eyes of the corpse were black, and rotted, with a blood-consistency liquid of purple/black draining from both eye sockets. The corpse lay face up, absent all its teeth. The mouth remained open, and I observed the tongue to be missing. Distinguishing characteristics still present allowed me to ascertain the gender of the victim. My conclusion is the victim died elsewhere, and the perpetrator or perpetrators used Ravens Cove as a dumping ground."

Kat looked up at Bart. "Purple and black? Yellow flesh?"

"Yep. Advanced decomp. Though I don't remember such a decayed state on a corpse where the body is still held together by muscle and tissue. And, you know what else is odd?"

Kat gave Bart a questioning look.

"He lay on Corpse Mound, at the opening to the ravine. I mean laid out just like the outline on the mound. Some sicko!" Bart shook his head in disgust. "So, lock your doors and windows, young lady! Not a suggestion—an order."

Kat's indignant eyes fired invisible arrows into Bart's.

"I pray this dirtbag has crawled back into whatever hole he came out of. If not ..." Bart's voice trailed off in thought. *If something happened to Kat, I'd never forgive himself.*

Kat stopped listening at "an order." Her thoughts turned to the legend handed down for centuries. She battled with herself about bringing up the story. She decided, took a deep breath and readied herself for the backlash to come.

"The legend of Corpse Mound has an eerie similarity to this."

"I can't see how a legend started in the 1700s is at all relevant here. I need information with a smidge more pertinence. This is no time for tales of goblins, witches, and dark things."

"You know there's more to it than goblins and witches." Kat locked eyes with Bart, daring him to defy her.

Bart snorted. "Right—and pigs fly!"

"What do pigs have to do with anything?"

"If you're questioning this death as supernatural, then for sure this is going to stir up the old tale about the ravine."

"What if it isn't just an old tale?"

"Stop. You are one of the most logical people I know, until it comes to this subject. Stop!"

"I'm just saying our ancestors' stories say these types of murders have happened again and again over the centuries and..."

"Stop! Those are legends, not fact. There is no black evil in the ravine! Those are scary stories parents use to keep their kids from going to dangerous places. No more! Now let's look for a flesh and blood suspect, shall we?"

Chastised and embarrassed, Kat turned and began typing.

The tarnished brass bell above the glass entry door clanged.

A disheveled, white-haired stranger stepped in.

"Can I help you?"

"Hope so. I'm new in town and need directions to the church."

"Well, there are two here. The oldest and most popular is the Congregational Alliance run by the Right Reverend Martin Plotno at the corner of Main and Willow."

The man grimaced, quick to replace it with a warm smile.

Kat dismissed the pained look as her imagination.

"No, ma'am, not the one at Main and Willow. Is there another?"

"There is a newer one. It's not as popular—a more fundamental church. Lots of fire and brimstone, and teaching from the Bible. The pastor, Paul Lucas, is a nice enough sort. By the way, what's your name?"

Maybe you are looking for a church in hopes of guilt-relief and forgiveness for leaving a decaying, stinky corpse in Ravens Cove before you go on the run, Kat thought.

"Josiah Williams." He gave a quick, short bow. He clutched a black-brimmed hat in his hands and held it at his waist.

"Well, Mr. Williams ..."

"Josiah, please. He bowed again, raised his head, and looked into her eyes. "I can feel we are going to be friends."

Alarm rose in Kat's gut. The last time she felt this way, the stray cat, dubbed BC, had just bitten her arm while she was trying to dress his open wounds.

"Well, Mr. Williams, if you are interested in the new church, it sits on Birch, just off Main. Take Main south until you get to Birch. Turn right. Birch takes you out of town. It's a long, uphill walk. Just keep going, and you'll run into the church before you reach the wetlands."

"Thank you, Katrina Agnes Tovslosky. Pastor Lucas's church is the one I seek."

"Wait! How do you know my name?"

The clang of the bell answered her.

"Rethinking locking my doors *and* windows," Kat murmured. "Look at the time!"

The clock read eleven or Zero eleven hundred, as Bart, the twenty-four-hour-clock-is-the-only-correct-time advocate would say.

Kat placed both hands over the keyboard and started typing.

"Hey KittyKat, thought I'd find you here," Wendy shouted in her ear.

Kat jumped, banging her knee hard against the desktop. "Ouch! Dang it Wendy!"

Wendy floated in front of Kat, placing her elbows on top of the computer monitor, ignoring Kat's obvious irritation.

"How's about lunch, girlfriend?"

"Busy here." Kat's eyes never left the report as she continued to type.

Wendy bent her head, to look at the computer screen upside down, long, copper curls cascading onto Kat's fingers and keyboard.

Kat grabbed a handful of the red-brown locks and pulled.

"Owwww." Wendy jumped back, frowned. She again put her elbows on top of the monitor.

"Come on; you know Jo's will be buzzing with the latest gossip!"

"No."

Kat raised her head and smiled up at Wendy. "If you're going to Jo's, I could use a big cup of coffee."

"Me too," Bart yelled from his office.

Wendy and Kat broke into simultaneous laughs.

"Fine, Bartster," Wendy yelled back, "but I expect to be reimbursed!"

"Right after you reimburse me for last week's lunch."

Wendy's lower lip came out in a false pout. She turned and sailed out the door.

"Doubt we'll see that cup of coffee," Kat yelled.

CHAPTER 2

A MAN ON A MISSION

Josiah Williams walked into the sun's warmth and made his way through the crowd still gathered in twos, threes, and fours.

"They say the body looked like a rag doll!"

"...drained of blood, flat as a pancake!"

Josiah slowed his pace, listening more closely.

"Purple and black oozing from the eyes."

The familiar pain of grief shot from his stomach to his heart. Tears spilled from Josiah's eyes, down leathery cheeks.

"O God, no, not again," he cried.

More bits and pieces of conversation bombarded his ears. Josiah became certain the destroyer of his own home, and his family so many years before, now resided here.

"Why here, O God? Why now?"

His strength waned. Josiah sat down on a bench. Behind the bench a sign read, "Cassie's Salon."

A 60-ish woman, just coiffed and smelling like salon chemicals, swept out of the salon's glass and wood door.

"Cassie never says a bad word about anyone. What a lamb she is, Ransom!" the older woman said to a younger woman with cherry Kool-Aid colored hair.

"Yes. Although, sometimes I wonder why she's so good and her life is such a wreck. Husband left her, estranged from her parents.

Why would those kinds of relationship troubles happen to such a friendly and sweet person?"

"Don't know. It is a shame."

Both women continued down Main, their conversation melting into the loud buzz on the street.

Josiah knew all things were not as they seemed.

"The hidden secrets destroy our souls," he whispered. "Just look at me. Not so long ago, or maybe very long ago, I was a drinking, laughing, jovial man who came home to a wife and children every night after relaxing at the local bar."

"'Nice fellow,' all my drinking friends said of me." He smirked.

"They did not know. I sure presented a kind persona to all who knew me. All but my own family, that is. With them, I became as mean-spirited and evil as I pretended to be pleasant and affable to my buddies.

"The day of my home's destruction, I didn't go home. Instead, I celebrated my big raise and flirted with Jane, the town's most available young woman. An hour later, the Devil paid a visit to my small hometown." Josiah wiped back the angry tears and stood up.

"What's done is done."

Convincing Pastor Lucas would not be easy. *It is never easy to speak of the spiritual realm in concrete terms, Josiah thought. Been there, done that, bought the whole outfit.* Josiah winced at the sad memory of one of his wife's many sayings. *I should know. Not very long ago my view of God and the spiritual world could be described as agnostic, at best.*

"My advantage is knowledge. I know Lucas is already fighting a battle with evil clothing itself as light and a friend of God. But how do I convince him of this fact, Lord?"

Josiah walked up Main toward Birch and took in the small mom-and-pop shops of Ravens Cove.

There stood the all-important General Store, which sold everything from bolts to TVs. Through the window, he could see a food aisle on the left—*better check the expiration date.*

The library sat across the street, the largest and newest building he had seen so far. It sat at the town's center amid dead-looking birch, mountain ash, and willow trees of late-autumn.

"Knowledge is a pride to this small town," he mused. "I wonder if wisdom is as well."

Next to the library, almost joined to it, stood the town hall, filling in the rest of the square. Only the library rivaled its ornate architecture. Two lions flanked either side of a large, arched doorway. Its grey concrete exterior made it oppressive.

Large, Greek-style planters sat in front of the lions, a few geraniums still fighting to maintain their scarlet colors, but losing the battle to the cold days and even colder nights. The crimson blooms underscored the coldness of the structure, giving it a most sinister look.

It's not just the way the building looks, Josiah thought. *It's the way the place feels.*

Josiah imagined how the green trees and beautiful flowers of spring and summer disguised the building's oppressiveness.

But just as light throws truth on what lies in the shadows, the bareness of October exposed the structure's personality. The building had a power of its own and dwarfed the larger structure to its right.

Josiah took his eyes off city hall and focused his attention on the rest of the street. People milled in front of the hardware store. He imagined it housed the essential odds and ends needed to keep a home or business in decent repair during the long winter to come.

A combined eatery and coffeeshop came next. The rich coffee aroma drifted back to Josiah on a light breeze as a customer opened the door, pulled on his coat, and started up Main.

Josiah shivered. The breeze chilled him, but his senses discerned something much more sinister in the air. His quickened his pace. *Time is shorter than I first thought.*

Josiah caught the unmistakable stench of iron and blood in the wind. A malicious snigger assaulted his mind's ear. He made a quick turn to his right and froze.

There, two storefronts ahead, a dark cloud oozed in a square mist from the minuscule area around the doorjamb of the blacked-out entry. The murky fog took form. It stood on two semitransparent limbs, like a man coming out from a crouch, and first walked, drifted, then walked again until it disappeared up Main.

Josiah looked at the sign over the door.

"Adults Only!" it shouted in bold, red lettering. Centered below the scarlet lettering in even larger writing the sign read, "The Trash Bin: Occult and New Age. Adult Entertainment Section."

Josiah turned back to Main and followed the dark being up the street. Where it stopped first shocked, then sent a vibrating terror through him.

The fog hovered at the door of the Congregational Alliance Church—right beside a placard stating, "We love all of you! Those who believe are saved, no matter your lifestyle. Come, join us!"

Josiah slowed his pace to study the blackness crowding the church's door. He watched as a mid-30s, red-haired, ruddy-skinned man walked through the foreboding shadow to unlock the church.

A wide grin replaced the grim, serious mouth in a flash. At the same time his neck rose, stiff, as if he looked down on this world, and no one knew better than he. He walked into the church.

"Is he lost, Lord?"

No answer.

Josiah shrugged. "Not surprising. The answers are not at my command." More often than not they came later rather than earlier in his missions.

Josiah started toward the long stairs to the church. He wanted to warn those inside of the destruction hanging over the place.

An unseen hand pushed on his chest, strong and gentle.

The command coursed through his heart. "No, Josiah. Today, this is not part of your battle."

Josiah hesitated, and then turned, fighting with every thread of his being to obey.

For the third time in a day, tears welled up in his topaz-blue eyes, spilling in silence down his weathered, lined cheeks. Memories and emotions flooded his mind. He smelled the burning flesh, and saw the deformed bodies. He grasped his elbows in both hands, bent over and dry-heaved.

"Why, Lord, must I wait? You can make me invincible so I can kill the thing which has killed my heart. Why must I continue to live and not have vengeance?"

Josiah's foot hung midair, ready to stomp the concrete. He stopped short and stood like a pelican in the water.

"Too old," he muttered. "Sure as life, I'd fracture something, and then who'd have a good laugh? An older body and a youthful mind are always in conflict.

"I know, Lord, vengeance is Thine," he whispered, and bowed in reverence to God.

Josiah's meeting with Pastor Lucas took on more urgency, and he quickened his pace.

Uniform, white homes with dark shutters replaced his view of the church building.

"Little houses on the hillside," he began to sing, remembering the old song about all houses being the same and made of ticky-tacky.

The town fell behind. The sidewalk ended, giving way to a rudimentary trail, full of dips and holes. He opted for a brush-covered, one-lane gravel road which looked less hazardous than the path. He observed several driveways going nowhere. They sliced into the thick brush, and ended ten feet in.

"Abandoned hopes or hopes for the future?" he wondered aloud.

Even in late-autumn, the tenacious green grass pushed its way through dry, brown leaves. Where no sun warmed it, the surrounding vegetation bent low under the weight of the night's frost.

"Did you send me on a wild-goose chase, Katrina?"

Josiah walked a bit farther. He spotted a small, dirty-white structure. He recognized it from his dreams—the dreams directing him to travel to Ravens Cove, so far from his home in what the locals here called the "Lower 48."

He proceeded up the paint-chipped wooden steps to a porch in similar disrepair. It looked to be about the same size, and from the same era, as most of the houses in Ravens Cove. What differentiated it from the others were the words over its door.

"Let all who enter here, enter to find salvation in the Truth, the Way and the Life, Jesus Christ."

Josiah smiled, and said a silent prayer for God to go before him so he, Josiah, would speak God's truth to this pastor, this shepherd for the Most High.

CHAPTER 3

VISIONS AND DISBELIEF

Paul Lucas spent a fitful night, a night full of violent visions and unseen foes. He rose early. *May as well get a head start on Sunday's sermon.*

Hours later, he still stared at a blank computer screen. *Nothing.*

Paul tiptoed from his desk to the closet, aware any movement would alert his resting spouse. Continuing in stealth-mode, he sneaked down the stairs, managing to avoid the one which always protested in a tone loud enough to wake the dead. The front door secure, Paul headed down the outdoor steps, and arrived at the small church he poured his heart and soul into over the past several months.

The Right Reverend Plotno and his "Elders" attacked Paul at every turn. His own congregation started to question the Word of God, and he didn't know why. His shoulders slumped in weariness.

Paul prayed, "Precious Jesus, grant me courage. Let my heart be at peace. You told us to give You our burdens. I feel like I have, Lord. So why am I so weary? Am I wrong to have come to Ravens Cove? Did I just imagine You wanted me to be here?"

Paul sighed, then continued, "Forgive me, God. I am a sinner and human; I am dust and I find comfort in the fact You know it and love me anyway. Help me to do Your will, O God. Help me, please."

The door squeaked open, reminding Paul of the need to oil it. The morning sun bathed the makeshift pews in golden light. Paul turned toward it and squinted into the brightness.

A man who looked to be in his 70s, or then again maybe in his early 50s, walked through the church door, purpose guiding his steps.

Josiah held out his hand as he approached Paul. "Reverend Lucas?"

Probably another of the Right Reverend's parishioners sent to discourage and maybe even threaten me. Anger colored his cheeks. He stood rigid, both hands at his sides.

"I am Paul Lucas. Not a reverend but a minister of God," he answered.

The Right Reverend Plotno used any instance to remind Paul and others of the fact Paul did not attend seminary. Paul's studies were through a Bible College in his hometown of Missoula, and those studies were by correspondence course. Somehow Plotno found out.

"You aren't a real minister," he said. "Correspondence school! You're a fake; people should send you packing!"

Remembering the Right Reverend's words tore a new hole in Paul's heart. *He may be right.* Paul's confidence plummeted to a new low. *I should have stayed in Missoula and worked the ranch.*

Paul focused on the man in front of him. "What can I do for you Mr ...?"

"Williams," Josiah continued to extend his hand, "but, please call me Josiah."

"What can I do for you Mr. Williams?"

Josiah sighed and lowered his hand. "I come on most urgent business. I have been sent to help you."

Cynicism replaced shame. "I've heard this before."

Erwin Ramsted, a staunch member of the Congregational Alliance, offered Paul a large sum of money to leave Ravens Cove and never return.

"To help with your moving expenses," he said.

It didn't work then, and it won't work now!

"I don't need the kind of help you're offering, Mr. Williams. Please leave. I have work to do."

"I have never come to offer you help before. I am here to talk to you about a matter of great import—a matter of life and death! We must speak. I have been sent by God!"

Paul believed in a more authentic scenario: This Josiah Williams represented a new attack by the CA'ers. Have the Bible thumper become involved with a loony commanded by God.

"I do not believe you. Go to the Right Reverend, and tell him this plan won't work either. Now, again, please leave!"

Josiah stood in silence, not taking his eyes off Paul.

The man's clear, transparent eyes caught Paul off guard. They reminded him of the rich blue of the sky on a crisp, cold, Ravens Cove day. He shook his head.

Josiah took a deep breath, "I do not know a Right Reverend. I do know a humble Jewish carpenter Who is my King, Who told me to come to this church in this town."

God, please provide wisdom, Paul prayed. He closed his eyes and took a deep breath.

"Maybe you are who you say you are, and God forgive me if I am wrong. If you are not associated with the Congregational Alliance, then you do not know how I have battled to establish this humble church in this town.

"If you are associated with them, then you know all too well the slander and schemes I have endured in the past months.

"All I know right now is I am not willing to risk disparagement of my family and this church. Now, please go!"

Josiah sighed again, heavier this time. *What now, O God?*

The answer came before he finished praying. *Revisit him tomorrow; he will understand more by then.*

Josiah turned to Paul. "I will return tomorrow. God bless your day with truth and understanding."

Josiah strode to the entrance and opened the door.

"I'd rather you didn't come back," Paul answered.

The noonday light outlined Josiah's frame with a bright silhouette. Paul watched the older man place the well-worn, black hat on his head, but not until he cleared the threshold.

As the door closed, Paul caught a glimpse of a second man standing so close to Josiah they could have been one. His height dwarfed the old man's tall frame. An electric-blue light swirled and danced with each man's movement.

Paul shook his head to clear his vision. *Just what I need, to start hallucinating angelic beings!*

A whisper with the strength of a thousand stallions plowed through the cynicism making a home in his heart. "Not a hallucination, Paul, but a vision."

Relief and hope flooded Paul. Yet as quickly as those feelings rose, he pushed them from his consciousness. *Where has hope gotten me?*

Paul remembered arriving in Ravens Cove full of a small child's optimism. He learned the devastation of crushed dreams and innocence born from the naïve belief those who professed to follow Jesus Christ told the truth.

I will not make the same mistake twice," he vowed.

CHAPTER 4

DARK AND LIGHT

The Right Reverend Plotno hummed a happy tune in his grand church, his kingdom, as he liked to think of it.

"I'm on the right track. The elation I experienced on the way into the church proves it."

To make the day even better, he heard from his favorite parishioner, the delectable Anita Conner.

Stop, Plotno. You are a married man! he thought. *As if such a small fact would keep my libido in check.*

Anita reported to him on the dreadful Paul Lucas. "He's wearing down, Right Reverend. I went to one of his services, as you requested."

She smiled wickedly and continued, "So few in attendance. The ones who were there are ancient and can't even stand up for the worship songs."

Plotno took the opportunity to pull her into his arms and hold her just a bit longer than needed. "Paul Lucas, and the days of his nightmare of a church, are almost over!"

Anita nodded. "How I hate the place! His sermons make me feel guilt and shame!"

Anita didn't tell Plotno there were a few new faces in church on Sunday, younger ones, with small children playing at their feet or in the chairs next to them. Such information would only upset him. And she wanted nothing to upset him.

Plotno released Anita.

"Lucas is a fanatic and a danger to my people," he said while pacing back and forth in front of the altar.

He stopped ... and turned blazing eyes to Anita. "All he does is make people feel guilt and shame over accepting each other's actions. So what if people embrace adultery and worship angels or nature? Jesus was a wise man, well-known for His radicalism 2,000 years ago. What makes our congregation's practicing what used to be taboo and is now tolerated, even accepted by society, any different?"

"I know," Anita answered. "Jesus's message of the consequences of sin and the need for repentance are outdated. Love means acceptance. It means complete tolerance. Love always feels good because pleasure and love are synonymous."

Plotno touched her cheek. "Correct. So, as you know, sin does not exist."

"He's getting what's coming to him. Lucas doesn't look like he's sleeping well, Reverend. Big circles under his eyes and deep lines on his young face." Anita's voice fluctuated in a mock tune. "Can't be good."

"His comeuppance can't come soon enough."

Anita raised smoldering, hooded eyes to Plotno's cold, grey-black ones. She longed to bury herself in his arms and watch those cold eyes turn warm as she nibbled his neck.

Plotno held her gaze for a moment, then turned his eyes to the stained-glass window sending rainbows of color into the sanctuary.

"Seminary taught me to forgive, but there will be none for Paul Lucas! He teaches the wrong message, one which will destroy any tolerant, progressive church. 'All are saved by faith not by works.' Horrible thinking! Lucas quotes nonstop from the Bible. He's just as outdated as it is!

"Why would people attend a church, except to ensure salvation? They only need to attend church services every Sunday and Wednesday and give as much money to the Congregational Alliance as they can. And, most importantly, listen to my instructions because I am their spiritual guide. Then, they will be saved."

"Yes, Reverend."

He turned his attention back to Anita and caressed her arm. "Such good news about the horrid little church."

A thrill coursed through her body, bringing instant color to her cheeks. Reverend Plotno brushed back a stray hair sticking to Anita's eyelashes. She shivered in response.

He smiled into her love-struck eyes, and then released her gaze. "You are a true asset to this congregation."

Plotno turned to the altar to review his notes for Wednesday's sermon.

He turned back. "One more thing. I know how much you hate going there and listening to the blather Lucas is spewing. But, dear one, I need you to go again."

Anita deflated like a balloon.

Plotno lifted Anita's chin, fixing his eyes on hers. "Be strong, and you will be rewarded!"

She touched his arm. "Not again, please."

His heart quickened in response, thinking of what would come. "Yes, again," he whispered as he bent to her ear, "this time, and anytime I ask you to. You know obedience is as important as tolerance." He nibbled her ear.

Anita's knees weakened from his touch. She surrendered and hung her head. "All right."

"Good girl. Now off with you, I must plan for tonight's study."

Anita Conner turned, not sure if her unsteady legs would hold her weight. She tried a step. Reassured her limbs were okay, she strode to, and out, the heavy, carved wood doors.

"This day is feeling *fanta*stic," the Right Reverend mused, "fantastic, indeed."

The church door swung open for the second time.

Plotno spoke without turning. "What is it now?"

An unfamiliar voice boomed through the silence of moments before. "Your destruction is imminent. Stop now, for your sake and the sake of your congregation!"

Martin Plotno whirled in response, holding a candle extinguisher like a sword, ready to confront the intruder. A thin, white-haired, unshaven specter of a man stood before him.

Lowering his weapon, Plotno said, "There is a soup kitchen down the street, old man. They can help you. There's nothing for you here. Come back when you clean yourself up."

"I am sent to help you, sir."

"Really? Who thinks I need any assistance you can offer? More to the point, which congregant put you up to this?"

"I know—Erwin! Go tell him I preferred the stripper in the birthday cake."

"The God of Jacob and Isaac sent me, Martin Plotno, Who says to you, 'Stop using Me and my Christ to lead others astray. Obey *Me*. Worship the one true God.'

"You are in a teacher's position, pretending to be a man of God, and woe to you!"

"What would you know about God? You don't even know enough to take a proper bath!"

"God spoke through James in the New Testament, Mr. Plotno: 'Not many of you should presume to be teachers, my brothers, because you know that we who teach will be judged more strictly.' Change, I plead with you, or your destruction is imminent."

Anger rose in Plotno's throat. "How dare you—an example of bad hygiene and a disciple of the streets—speak to me in such a way!

"Do not step any farther into this sacred place, you sick old man. Get out! We don't allow your kind here!"

Josiah held his ground. "I am a servant of the one true God, sent to give you this warning. May God have mercy on you!"

Josiah turned, cocked his head as if listening to an unseen voice and turned back to Plotno.

"I have been instructed to clear something up for you. Whether you believe it or not, there is a Hell and not all go to Heaven, even though our God does not will any to perish. You are deceived and, again I say, repent!"

Josiah marched to the back of the church, lifting his hand, waving it back and forth to part the black mist covering the door.

It shot to one side before he walked through, a dark curtain blown by an invisible wind.

The dark mist, Atramentous by name, vibrated with hatred, then fear at what he saw. An angel of God stood beside this man.

"Uriel!"

The angel turned and nodded. "Atramentous."

Atramentous bent his head to avoid the blinding light. After they passed, he raised his head, formed an invisible mouth, a deep red chasm where the black mist had been. A guttural, gurgling roar spewed out to sound the alarm, sending sleeping birds flying into the sky crying in terror.

No response.

"Now what?" he pondered.

A cunning demon, Atramentous carried out Iconoclast's orders with ease. His ability to plan, though, bordered on nonexistent. After a laborious mental exercise, a vicious smile broadened the black line of a mouth.

"I know how to warn Iconoclast, and receive a commendation for my abilities to devise a strategy."

Atramentous slid from the church door and retraced his earlier path up Main.

CHAPTER 5

THE ULTIMATUM

Atramentous slithered under the door of the new-age shop, wrapped his semitransparent bulk around Miggie and spoke, "Get word to the one who allows you to have this place. The very one who has prospered you. The plan to complete the Congregational Alliance's good work is under attack."

"What do you want me to do?"

I have no patience with this idiot. Atramentous shifted his form to a misty, black rope and tightened.

Miggie gasped for air and pulled at the invisible bindings for relief.

In a fluid, violent motion, Atramentous released him.

Miggie fell to the floor, heaving.

He found breath enough to whisper, "Forgive me, great one. I am but a human. Please instruct me." He dropped into a prone position, face down.

How I hate this mortal, Atramentous thought. *I should just finish him!* He started to tighten around Miggie again, then relaxed.

Iconoclast's instructions were clear. "You can have him when I say; no sooner. Until then do not harm him or you will be no more!"

Atramentous's desire to destroy Iconoclast rose to a feverish level, threatening to make him forget his assignment.

His fear of Iconoclast and those loyal to the Commander flooded him, acting as a tranquilizer, and squelched his desire for battle.

He spoke to Miggie. "Go to the top of Ravens Ravine at sunset. Do not enter the ravine."

"No, there are too many police! I will be questioned and become a suspect!"

"Fool. Go to Ravens Ravine at sunset or die now!" Atramentous tightened around Miggie again, compressing Miggie's bones.

Miggie cried out. Small capillaries broke in his eyes. The mounting pressure made him feel as if his eyes would pop like over-filled balloons; he heard a distinct crack as something in his body gave way to the constraints.

Atramentous released him and again Miggie fell to the floor, this time wailing in fear and pain.

"Shut up and heed my instructions: Go to the top of Ravens Ravine. Call down these words, 'I am a messenger sent by your great guard who protects the Congregational Alliance.'

"Then continue with, 'Your great guard says there is one who has come to this place, your place, who means to destroy you. He is strong in the Holy One and is accompanied by Uriel. You destroyed his family, and he seeks revenge. But, O great one, no one can defeat you. Your messenger awaits your command.'

"Sit down, cross-legged, facing away from The Corpse Mound. You will be instructed. Until you are told what to do, be quiet, be still, and do not venture onto the ravine path. If you do any of these things, you will die."

"As you say!"

Satisfied, Atramentous stretched out, slid along the floor, under the door and down the street to his post.

The Commander would be irate, he thought. *It is good this creature will be delivering the news.* Atramentous shivered. The initial anger of the Commander could be unrestrained.

If Miggie becomes a sacrifice, so be it. I do want to crush the pipsqueak into dust, but rather he meet the Commander's punishment than me.

Satisfied with his plan, Atramentous settled his charcoal bulk over the door and awaited Iconoclast's mandate.

CHAPTER 6

A SECRET LIFE

A troubled and frightened Miggie busied himself unpacking and inventorying his latest books, potions, crystals, and adult play paraphernalia. Terror toyed with his mind until it became like a guitar string tightened to the breaking point.

The back door to Miggie's shop popped open, sounding like a gunshot. Miggie jumped up from his kneeling position and stumbled backward, tripping over a box. He plopped like a sack of flour to the floor, legs in an upside-down *V*, arms outstretched behind him.

He strained his neck upward, squinting into the blinding light. Shifting all of his weight to his right arm, Miggie threw the left one over his eyes as a shield. He recognized the familiar form of one of his best customers, the alluring and demure Anita Conner.

Miggie distributed keys for the alley entrance to his top customers, including Anita. His patrons appreciated the thoughtfulness. Miggie made much more money from this good business policy. *A true win-win,* he thought.

"A little jumpy today, Miggie?"

"Got to get the door fixed; sounds like a bomb exploding every time it opens."

He pushed himself vertical in one motion.

Anita studied him for a while, noticing the redness of his eyes and a nasty purple bruise rising on his right cheek. "If you say so."

"Looking for something in particular?"

"Well, needing a potion, I think, maybe a spell book or two ..." Anita's voice trailed off as she headed for the occult section across the room. She touched each book with her right index finger, reading as she went.

"You'd think working in a library you could have all this at your disposal," he swept his arm from right to left, "cheaper, too."

"Indeed; if I want all of Ravens Cove to question my bringing in those kinds of books. There are some big eyes watching the library and me!" Anita said with disgust.

Miggie stared, taking a moment to admire her backside, and then shrugged. *Whatever,* he thought, *to each his or her own. We are encouraged to be tolerant.*

"Here we go." She hefted two large volumes of chants, spells, and curses in her arms.

"Now the makings of a potion or two." Anita thumbed through the books to find what she wanted, placed the massive volumes on the counter, and walked off to Miggie's version of a grocery store, grabbing the items needed for her purposes. She paid Miggie and headed toward the back entrance.

"I'll go first. Just in case there are prying eyes," Miggie said.

"Appreciated."

Miggie pulled open the gunshot contraption of a door, stepped out into the alley and looked both ways. No one in sight.

A garbage lid fell to the ground. Miggie swung his hands up over his ears to muffle the deafening rattle and scrutinized the garbage cans and immediate area. "Stupid alley cats."

After another quick inspection of the alley, Miggie said, "It's safe."

Anita tipped her head to Miggie and stepped into the alley, humming under her breath, pleased with her new acquisitions. Now her love interest would not escape!

She glanced at her watch. The potions would have to wait until the library closed. Then, she could pursue her true passion—Martin Plotno.

Josiah Williams headed into the alley behind the Trash Bin. He heard as clear as day, "Stop and watch!" He did.

He observed a young, dark-haired woman exit the Trash Bin's back door and proceed to the opposite end of the alley.

Josiah turned and walked back to Main Street. This part of the puzzle dropped into his mental box, and joined the other unexplained pieces.

The October sun, although just two o'clock, stretched the building's shadows like rubber bands at the breaking point, heralding the coming night.

Exhaustion overtook Josiah and weakened his spirit, mind and body. *In this state, I'll be in grave danger if I stay out past nightfall. Even though the evil is not yet at full strength, or even quarter strength, I cannot chance crossing its path.*

"Time to find a room, some food, and get cleaned up."

Caitiff, Iconoclast's star spy, watched the old man leave the alley. He smiled, wicked yellow-black razors jutting from the gaping hole of a mouth. "The old man! What a great prize for Iconoclast."

He raced into the sky, small, black wings carrying him to the ravine.

CHAPTER 7

NO IS NOT AN OPTION

"I'm not getting anywhere on this report!" Kat yelled over the incessant ringing of the telephone. The phones warbled, almost nonstop, since she arrived.

"Do what you can," Bart answered.

"Don't I always?"

"Yes. And I thank you."

"Right—Sheriff's office." Kat struggled to keep her greeting civil. "Can I help you?"

"Hey, KittyKat, how 'bout a late lunch?"

"Wendy, I am up to my eyeballs here. Lunch isn't in the plan." She cradled the phone between her neck and shoulder as she tried to get another word of the report typed.

"Told you. Something big, huh?"

"You know I can't discuss an investigation in progress," Kat said for what she felt like the thousandth time.

This game began in first grade. Kat tried to keep a secret, Wendy wheedled it out of her after a long tug-of-war and matching of wits. Wendy sang to the world, "Kat's in love with *Jimmmy*," or "Kat's a scaredy-cat and thinks there's monsters in her *roooom*."

"Not even one itsy, juicy detail?"

And here we go again! Wendy still thinks we're in first grade and makes it part of her life's work—when she takes a break from creating beautiful glass objects in her studio or her newest romantic interest—to cajole the secrets out of me. Kat smiled. Since coming to work at the sheriff's office, Wendy had batted a big fat zero.

"Back off, woman. If you want to be a good friend, bring me that cup of coffee from Jo's. I'm going to be at this for quite a while."

"Fine," Wendy said, "just fine and go ahead and be closed mouthed, Ms. Secret Sally."

The line went dead.

"Who's on the phone, Kat? Another busybody?"

"Yep. Now about this report ..."

The phone shrilled again.

"Oh, for the love of Pete! Sheriff's office, can I help you?" A *how dare you interrupt me again* tone underscored the polite question.

A deep resonate voice answered her. "Sheriff Andersen, please."

Kat launched into the monologue for the press. "If you are calling for an interview, the sheriff does not have the time today or tomorrow. We are preparing a press statement for release. Thank you for your patience." *And Wendy wonders why I don't enjoy chatting on the phone. One day like this, and she'd know why!*

The phone left her ear to return to the cradle. She caught, "Not a reporter," and debated about hanging up anyway.

"Shoot!" Kat brought the phone back to her ear. "Then what can we do for you?"

"I am Kenneth Melbourne with the Anchorage unit of the FBI. It is imperative I speak with Sheriff Andersen."

Knowing how Bart felt about outside interference in his investigations, and because he was up to his ears in this one, Kat went into protective mode.

Not in a month of Sundays, Mr. FBI, she thought but responded in a sweet tone. "The sheriff is in meetings all day. Can I take a message?"

"Interrupt his meeting, and get him to the phone. I need to speak to him now."

His arrogant tone became the proverbial straw.

"I'm sorry, Mr. Melbourne, is it?"

"Agent Kenneth Melbourne."

Kat continued in the sickening-sweet tone which always preceded the scathing, sarcastic tongue-lashing she became famous for in Ravens Cove.

"Agent Melbourne, then. Sheriff Andersen is in the midst of a murder investigation. He does not have time to break away from his meetings to talk to you. Am I clear now?" Not waiting for a response, "Good. Have a nice day."

Kat returned the phone to its home. "The gall of some people."

Riiiiing. Riiiiing.

"Darn instrument!" She took a deep breath. *No reason to go into Kat-fight mode with an unsuspecting person at the other end.*

"This is Agent Melbourne again. If you hang up, I will call back as many times as it takes. This is urgent. Tell your boss to pick up the phone, and do it now!"

Kat-fight mode sounded the first bell in the back of her brain. She knew her orders, and she would enforce them.

"With all due respect, Agent, no." She dropped the phone into the cradle.

Ten minutes and several Melbourne calls later, Kat stomped to Bart's office, angry at being ordered by the know-it-all FBI agent to get her "boss."

Bart looked up to blazing eyes and a flushed face. He leaned back in his chair, linking his hands behind his head, and hoping his body language would diffuse the onslaught of emotion. It didn't.

"There is an Agent Melbourne who keeps calling. He *insists* on talking to you."

"Told you my policy on nosy outsiders."

Being reprimanded brought the stew of frustration, weariness and hunger to a boil.

"Yes," her voice rose, "yes you have. And, *I* told him, too. And *I* hung up. And he called back again, and again, and again. *I* hung up *again*, and *again* and AGAIN. He is now ordering me, under threat of interfering with FBI business, to put my 'boss' on the phone. He is on hold."

Bart knew Kat. No matter who paid her, she did not have a "boss." She had been, and always would be, a freethinker and free spirit. He could not control the grin creeping across his mouth.

"I see you, Bartholomew Andersen. This is *not* funny. Now pick up the phone. And I'm putting the other line on hold until I get your all-important report typed!" She whirled, strode to her desk and plopped down, making her point with a thud.

Bart sighed. *Those ruffled feathers will have to be smoothed or my life will be unbearable.*

He turned to the phone. "Sheriff Andersen."

"Thanks for interrupting your meeting, Sheriff."

"Make it quick, Agent Melbourne, is it? I have a busy schedule."

"I believe I can be an asset to your investigation."

Bart seethed. Another one who thought him to be a small-town hick who couldn't find a key in a door lock. "Is that so?"

"I have worked on several serial murder cases prior to moving to Anchorage. In fact, it is my specialty. It looks like you might have the beginnings of one there. I would like to come and work the case."

"And I'd like to have summer in January, Agent Melbourne, but neither of them are going to happen. We're doing just fine. Thanks for your concern. If I need help in the future, I'll know who to call. Until then, goodbye." Bart hung up.

Ken looked at the phone. Shocked by the sheriff's blatant hostility, and realizing he once again listened to a dial tone, he hung up.

He turned his attention to the scenery beyond the window of his cubicle—*at least I have a window*—and mused at the Chugach Mountains in the east, hoping for inspiration. Dark brown peaks contrasted by snow which never melted, stood high and majestic in the background. Some were jagged and wild, while others were rounded and domestic. They should have given him pause to reflect on nature's magnificence. Instead, those mountains were a constant reminder of a life left behind.

How I hate living here. This place is quiet, which equals boring ... drug dealers, some murders, an occasional bank robbery and always gangs. I will return to California. This case in Ravens Cove is my way out.

He picked up the phone and dialed. "I need to talk with the chief, Marcy. Will you find some time in his schedule for me?"

This new guy, Marcy thought, *is one of my favorites. He's smart, kind, and handsome. What else could a single woman want? Of course, I'll help. Maybe get a date out of it!*

"Let me see ... how about three today?"

"Works for me. See you then and thanks."

Ken busied himself with the various alerts on his desk. Too antsy to concentrate, he strolled to the coffee room. When he returned fifteen minutes later, the message light glowed red. He listened to the message, secured the phone on his shoulder and dialed, all the while trying to shrug the free arm into his navy-blue jacket. On the third ring, Marcy picked up.

"I'm on my way."

He pushed his other arm into the jacket and jogged up the three flights of stairs to the chief's office. With the right pitch, he could be in Ravens Cove no later than tomorrow morning—sooner if he had his way.

CHAPTER 8

DAY'S END

Kat put the final touches on the sheriff's report. A statement which should have taken an hour took four because of the nonstop phone calls and visits from horrified Ravens Cove residents.

To Kat's relief, the media storm did not materialize. They believed Bart's watered-down version of the homicide, so the related phone calls stopped. For the time being, the media believed John Doe's death to be a tragic and all-too-familiar fate for the homeless.

Wendy's promised cup of coffee never arrived, and Kat felt in dire need of a pickup. Coffee and maybe a nice oversize chocolate chip cookie, made fresh at Jo's Bakery.

"The lunch," Kat looked at her watch which read four minutes to six, "the supper of royalty. Maybe two chocolate chip cookies. I deserve them—what a stressful, crazy day."

Kat grabbed her coat. "Leaving."

"Lock your doors! I mean it."

"Yes sir!" Whether she would or not depended on how she felt once she got home.

Kat shrugged into her royal-blue anorak, checked her pocket for the matching knit gloves and headed for the door.

Six o'clock in Ravens Cove in October meant dark. She'd grab the coffee and cookies to go.

"I do feel uneasy about being out tonight, and the report did nothing to soothe my concerns." She shivered.

"Thank goodness, I didn't find the body. I'd be in therapy for years! Which would be tough," she mused, "as there are no therapists in Ravens Cove."

Grandma Bricken comes close. Moose stew and sourdough bread fixed everything. Kat smiled and strolled north on Main to Jo's.

Kat opened the glass door. The crowd and its noise almost blew her over.

From autumn to spring, most of Ravens Cove residents were home by now. Not tonight. Too much fear and excitement about the day's happenings.

Kat braced herself and walked in.

Jo, actually, Josephina Latrell, walked briskly—for her bulk—from one customer to the next, taking orders. Coffee, sandwiches, no soup left.

Kat smiled. "A chip off the ole grandma block."

"Who's next?" Jo called out.

All business in a rush, the flushed Josephina made eye contact with each customer. During the off months, she would have closed this shop an hour earlier. Always one to see the opportunity, she remained open.

Life-long resident Carlton Jonas, having left his teens behind just a moment ago, stepped forward and placed his order.

Kat studied the blackboard on the wall behind the counter, which changed daily, depending on Jo's mood.

Chocolate chip cookies were not on the menu; Snickerdoodles were. Fine, a couple of Snickerdoodles and a mocha would be her evening's repast.

She noted the daily special—baked salmon roast. *Must be older than dirt by now. I'll see if Jo will give me some for BC.*

Having been housebound all day, BC would pounce in an instant.

After a painful trial-and-error period in which Kat's legs started to resemble a climbing post, she learned. Fish mollified BC. The trick: open the takeout box and slide it in the front door with the broom from the porch. BC couldn't resist salmon. He forgot to attack. Problem solved.

The teenager-man, Carlton, finished his order. The man who stepped to the counter next didn't reside in Ravens Cove. Kat released her cell phone from the pouch on her belt and dialed the sheriff's office.

"Yes, Kat." Bart knew her number by heart. He'd sure dialed it plenty of times when he needed emergency help.

"I'm at Jo's," she whispered.

"Speak up. I can't hear you."

Kat left her place in line, her stomach protesting, and walked to the door.

"I'm at Jo's."

"Good, bring me a sandwich, would ya? It's going to be a late night."

Kat sighed. "Bart, listen! There's someone down here I've never seen before. About six feet, thirtyish, red and black check flannel shirt, shiny, new blue jeans. With all of today's happenings, thought you might want to check him out."

"You're right. On my way. Order me a sandwich, okay?"

Heaven help me.

Kat made it to the counter in record time, placed her order, and took the opportunity, provided courtesy of the mirror hanging behind Jo's counter, to keep an eye on the stranger.

He sat in one of the coveted window-seats, and he looked like he would be staying for a while.

Having finished his meal, he focused on a day-old Anchorage newspaper, making him stick out like a sore thumb. Almost no one in Ravens Cove wanted to read the big town's newspaper. Which meant almost no one subscribed to it. If this guy wanted to fly under the radar, it would have been better to pick up one of the freebies outside the bakery.

The door opened, the night's frigid air rushed in with it.

Bart Andersen entered in one, quick step.

"Man, it's getting cold!" Bart said, rubbing his hands together.

He made his way through a now thinned-out line at the counter to Kat. "What, no sandwich yet?"

Kat narrowed her eyes and said, "Just made it to the counter."

"Kidding, Katrina, just kidding." He poked her with his elbow. "Now where's this person of interest?"

Kat motioned, right index finger pointing behind a cupped left hand, hidden by her body, in the direction of the man who appeared to be absorbed in his newspaper. The tightness of his body, and his jaw flexing now and again, contradicted the otherwise calm exterior.

"Order me the salmon salad sandwich and chips," Bart said as he moved out of line, and made a beeline to the stranger's table.

"Don't know you," Bart said to the back of the newspaper.

The stranger replied, "I don't know you either." He lowered his paper, piercing blue eyes locking into Bart's brown ones.

Bart stood straight, feet apart, hand on his holster. His stance spoke volumes about a man who meant business and wouldn't hesitate to take down a threat, when necessary.

The stranger rose and extended a hand. "Kenneth Melbourne. We spoke this morning."

A storm of anger darkened Bart's eyes until they were almost black. "I remember. I also remember telling you to stay away, yet here you stand! Care to explain, Agent Melbourne?" The way he emphasized *agent* made it sound like a dirty word.

Realizing his greeting would not be returned, Ken lowered his hand. *This isn't going to be easy, but the guy is going to have to accept I'm here for the investigation. Period.*

"I know we got off to a bad start this morning, Sheriff, but as I said, I'm here to help." These were the chief's words . . .

Instead of a three-o'clock conversation, Chief Binnings told Marcy to have Ken come along earlier.

Ken made his pitch. "I heard of a murder through one of my sources at the local paper, who received her information from who knows where. It's a real puzzle. Decaying body, but not dead long; colorful stuff oozing from the eyes. Odd positioning of the body. No fingerprints, no shoe treads—in fact, nothing to say anyone other than the victim came to the scene. It's possibly the work of someone who has killed before."

At first, the chief didn't give an inch. "Not our jurisdiction."

Ken pitched it hard. "I think this is the work of a serial killer, Andy."

He used the chief's first name when they were in private. He got to know Andy Binnings when they worked together in California, busting some high-profile bank robbers.

"And I think it could be the perpetrator crossed state lines. I mean, think about it, it's a town of a few thousand people. There has been nothing like this in Anchorage or any of the towns surrounding Ravens Cove. Where did he, or she, come from? It's worth looking into. We may have a real crazy on our hands here."

"Let's be honest, Ken. You're just itching to get out of here. But this one could blow up in our faces. Alaskans, as you know, aren't thrilled to have unrequested help.

"In addition, this sheriff already sounds like he is cocked to the make-a-complaint and make waves in the FBI, position."

Andy sat back and crossed his arms, never breaking eye contact with Ken. Coming to a decision, he sat up and thwacked his hands flat on the desk in front of him.

"Here's what I'll authorize. You can go to Ravens Cove. You have forty-eight hours to come up with facts, and I mean *solid* facts, Ken, to justify being there."

Ken jumped up, holding back the excitement to the best of his ability and headed for the door.

"One more thing, Agent."

Ken spun around to face the chief.

Binnings stood up, admonition in his eyes. "You will coddle this sheriff and handle him with kid gloves while you're at it. You are on shaky ground when it comes to jurisdiction. If a complaint materializes, it will get ugly for you, my friend."

"Understood. Thanks, you won't regret this!" Ken opened the door and sailed through.

"I better not, or it's your career," the chief shouted after him.

The backside of the door stopped the warning in its tracks . . .

Ken dropped back into the chair. "I am not here in an official capacity." *Yet.* "I am here to offer a helping hand." Ken almost choked on the last part. This man secured a place on Ken's bad side this morning with his stonewalling attitude. *I would like nothing better than to take complete control of the investigation, and leave you, good sheriff, in the dust of this Godforsaken hole of a town.*

"Here you go." Bart and Ken's attention turned to the warm, melodic voice.

A young—and gorgeous—work of God stood with one hand extended, holding a white lunch sack, toward the sheriff.

"Thanks." Bart smiled at her—the warmth of which showed the good sheriff harbored strong feelings for this magnet of a woman.

Ken made a mental note of a possible competitor.

I know this voice. Voices, after all, being one of Ken's specialties, gifts, as his auntie would have put it.

He could hear her now as if it were only yesterday. "A gift from the Lord Almighty, young man. He'll put it to good use for you one day, you wait and see."

And, whether Ken believed in the Lord Almighty or not, this talent helped to land the job in the FBI. *Go figure.*

"Do I know you?" Ken stood for a second time, extending his hand, to be rejected a second time. He dropped his arm. *Cold as glacier ice. The chill she puts off would freeze a lesser man.*

Kat raised her eyes, revealing their gold-flecked, sea green color. She shook her head.

"This is Agent Melbourne. You remember the FBI agent I spoke with this morning?"

Kat's look changed from cautious scrutiny to downright disdain in a twinkle.

She turned her attention to Bart. "I'll be on my way now. BC is going to make me pay for being late tonight."

Bart laughed. A warm, contagious sound, full of mirth and joy. "Yep, he harbors a grudge; I've got the scars to show it."

"By your own stubbornness! Who found the half-dead, scarred kitten, snatched him up in spite of the hissing and scratching, shoved it in a shoe box and brought him to me?"

"Guilty. And your love and care transformed BC into the cantankerous, ego-driven feline who became more of your close friend than a pet."

"True."

"Two peas in a pod, you two cats," Bart mused. Both were independent, both were semi-wild, and neither of them would be tamed.

If Kat weren't his first cousin, he'd marry her. Those qualities said 'real woman' to Bart Andersen.

Kat twirled on one foot and headed to the door. "I'm off to face the black tornado."

"Hold up! I'm walking you home. Don't even think of arguing with me tonight." Bart held up his hand. "Not a word! You know I'm right.

"We're finished here. Right, Mr. Melbourne?" Bart underscored Melbourne's unwelcome presence by discarding the title of Agent. He hoped the guy would take a hint. The jibe found its mark.

Ken ignored it. "For tonight, Sheriff, for tonight. I want some time to collect my thoughts. I'll be checking into the inn down the way."

Bart shot a disapproving glare at Ken before he moved away, put his hand on Kat's back and walked out the door into the bitter-cold night.

"What arrogance, coming to our town when you told him, in no uncertain terms, to stay away." Kat turned to look through the window of Jo's. "I don't like him one bit!"

Bart smiled. No one messed with Kat's family, friends, or anyone she considered her family or friends. "You are one of the most protective people I know."

"I am. And I'm proud of it."

"He's just another groupie, of a different kind. Wants to get in on the action and make a name for himself." Bart chuckled. "Boy, did he come to the wrong town. To make a name for himself, he needs information. I've lived here all my life and no one wants to talk to me when I'm on duty. Let him try."

Bart's mood lightened, and he began whistling a favorite childhood tune.

Kat joined in, dancing a jig to the melody of *Mares Eat Oats and Does Eat Oats and Little Lambs Eat Ivy*.

They broke into raucous laughter, turning heads as they headed south on Main to Kat's home.

CHAPTER 9

THE DARKNESS GROWS

Miggie made two trips to Ravens Ravine before sunset. On his first trip, he arrived well before the appointed time. He found the ground on corpse mound soiled from the body removed earlier in the day. He hurried back to his shop, grabbed an old blanket and ran back to the ravine. Both times, he sneaked under the yellow tape, hoping no one saw him violate the crime scene.

Feeling a bit foolish, but not so foolish as to ignore Atramentous's instructions, he threw down the blanket, and sat cross-legged, back to the ravine. He could feel the ice-cold ground beneath him. He shuddered at the thought of what might be seeping into his pants.

Focus, Miggie my man, focus.

He cleared his throat. "I am a messenger of your great guard. Please do not harm me, but listen to his warning. One is in Ravens Cove who means to destroy you. He is strong in God. He is working to muster God's people. You destroyed his family and, except for this man and a few others, his entire town. O great one, no one can defeat you. Tell me how you want to proceed to guarantee your victory. I await your instructions."

Miggie sat still, his chattering teeth piercing the otherwise silent countryside. He felt a presence.

To make matters worse, the lone hag tree appeared to be bending toward him. He used every bit of his self-control to stay immobile and to stifle the scream constricting his throat. Numb terror blanketed

Miggie's brain. He did not register the blood trickling from his mouth, or the self-inflicted wound on his tongue.

The old hag tree started to shimmer, exuding a tarnished-gold light.

Terror gave way to curiosity.

The sounds of long-dead leaves, none on this tree as long as he'd been alive, engulfed him. He covered his ears because the noise became unbearable.

"Stop," he yelled.

Miggie heard a gallows-laugh before the clatter of the ghost-leaves died. He dropped his hands.

The pale light illuminated, and then spotlighted, a small arrowhead sitting at his feet. Arrowheads were commonplace in Ravens Cove and not a remarkable find. Still, he could not stop looking at it.

It began to kaleidoscope through purple and black and red and even the jaundiced yellow of the tree. The rhythmic pulsation of the colors hypnotized him.

Miggie inched his fingers toward the arrowhead, making sure the rest of his body stayed statue-still.

Pain seared through his left hand. He opened it to find a deep cut, so deep Miggie saw bone before blood filled the gaping wound. The pain subsided. A scar, the color of eggplant, running in a straight line from his middle finger to the base of his hand remained.

It did happen! Miggie thought.

Miggie gazed into the magical stone. For the second time, Miggie broke the rule of silence. "This charm can wound and heal! With this new find, I can run Ravens Cove. I can rule all of Southcentral Alaska, then all of Alaska, and maybe even the world! The possibilities are endless!

"You'll all see! Reverend Plotno will be my minion, part of *my* new congregation."

A sallow light snaked from the arrowhead in his hand, dancing toward his chest, the macabre rhythm set to his heartbeat. A long tendril of ochre mist shot through his body, then pulled out.

Miggie stood, turned, and faced the ravine path. A wind, laced by the stench of decay, smacked him in the face. Instead of acting as a repellent, it acted as a magnet and drew him to the head of the path.

Breaking the rules emboldened Miggie. He took a step onto the path.

The anemic glow brightened and exposed once-invisible hag trees along the trail's edge. The trail ended at a treed archway.

A gnarly, misty finger shot down the pathway, pointing to the door. "I can't go down there! It's forbidden!"

"Run!" his mind commanded.

Desire overpowered his fear and collapsed under the relentless craving to know the guardian's secret of knowledge and power.

"This is why the guardian told me not to go! Well, turnabout's fair play, as they say. I know the secret now, and I will be free from the wretched fiend who proclaimed himself a friend, and is nothing of the sort. I will destroy him!"

Miggie advanced to his destiny, a smile on his face at the revenge he would exact on Atramentous.

Atramentous snapped alert. The deep, golden oak door of the Congregational Alliance began to bleed. Small, uniform tendrils coursed down its ornate top to its elaborate threshold. A roar of rage, smelling of burnt flesh and thousands of decaying, murdered souls, issued from the dark mist.

Miggie existed no more.

"The stupid mortal should have been my reward! Now, I won't taste the sweet nectar of the terror and pain when I drain the life from the pastry bag of flesh. Stolen. My prize stolen."

To make matters worse, Atramentous could not retaliate. The Commander would not abide even the appearance of rebellion.

He quieted. The blood crept back up the door and withdrew into the overhead.

Better him than me, thought Atramentous while he settled again over his post.

CHAPTER 10

GRIEVOUS MEMORIES

Josiah Williams awoke with a start from a fitful sleep. Dread-filled memories crowded his dreams. He played with his beloved Martha and Ezra, loving, innocent children who adored him, no matter how long he stayed away from home. They were in his arms again. He smelled those sweet children, just fresh from a bath, ready for a good night's sleep.

A murky mist engulfed them and pulled. They screamed, small arms reaching, reaching. Then, their lifeless bodies were tossed at his feet, like rag dolls. Dead where such life had been before.

Josiah's body heaved in uncontrollable sobs. "Why didn't you take me, Lord? Why my babies; why my wife?"

Josiah willed himself silent. He never received an answer. No matter how many times he beseeched God.

They were in heaven with Him now; Bonnie's belief in Jesus Christ unshakeable to the end. A model example to him, an agnostic leaning toward atheism, during their marriage. Oh, how she tried to make him see the truth. She stuck with him, and by him, throughout all the years of his neglect.

She raised those babies, not me.

Josiah felt an odd comfort in knowing the children and she were together in heaven. *No more pain or terror now, not for them.* They were in the hands of the One who sustained them through him and his coldness. They were drenched in God's warmth and love—a father's love he came to know too late.

In the irony of God, the day I chose to die, in fact, the day I held a gun held to his right temple, I found life, Josiah mused.

"Don't do it, Josiah," rang through his head. "The living God exists. He wants you. He will avenge your children, your beloved wife."

Of all the ideas to run through his mind, the story of Job came to mind while he held the cold steel to his temple.

"He, too, lost his family," Josiah remembered thinking. "But, unlike me, Job continued to proclaim God's sovereignty and goodness. And, just like Job, I prayed for death—for the misery to end. And, just like Job, I still live."

The story was enough to make Josiah lay the pistol down beside him. *What if I'm wrong?* The doubts and questions made him resolve putting off death by his own hand to a later time. Maybe an hour or maybe a day.

"In my arrogance, I told God, 'When the pain becomes unbearable, God, I will take my own life.'"

Then the thought, "And if I don't believe in You, why am I talking to You?"

Josiah's belief took hold. A seed in shaky, loose soil but a seed just the same.

Josiah walked to the window while consumed in the memory of his first encounter with salvation. He stared without seeing the darkness beyond.

The cold emanating through the under-insulated window sent a shudder through him, and he returned to the present.

He noted the darkness, and the absence of the forecasted full moon.

The thing has taken another victim and has grown stronger. Minister Lucas must hear me!

Josiah fell to his knees. "God, help Your servant; I have sinned. But You say if I repent You will wash me clean. Forgive me, Lord. You have ordained my days. You have ordained my purpose, O gracious God. Send Your holy angels before me; I cannot bend the ear of Paul

Lucas to what is happening here, but, You can, O Lord. Please hear my prayers. In Your mighty Son Jesus's name. Amen."

Josiah thought, "Maybe this death will work for good, Lord? Maybe the Thing will show itself sooner rather than later? Maybe this town could be rid of it before the evil from without feeding on the evil within the town, takes hold and destroys it?"

Josiah knew these current deaths were just the appetizers. The town would be the main course and the believers the sweetest of desserts.

A sudden urgency replaced his hope. Even in his town, the thing did not move at this speed. He rose and headed for the door.

Josiah caught a glimpse of himself in a mirror. Shaggy, unkempt grey hair sprouted above his ears and around his head like a weathered bird's nest. The wrinkles on his trousers and shirt evidenced yesterday's attire.

"Won't do much good to meet with Pastor Lucas if he thinks I can't even take care of myself."

Josiah turned to his right and into the bathroom to grab a shower and fresh clothing.

CHAPTER 11

A TENUOUS TRUCE

Kat opened her eyes to find herself staring into black glittering ones, catching a red glow. She screamed, and then covered her mouth.

BC placed a velvet black paw on her cheek, as if to comfort her, then turned two fluid circles and melted as only a cat can, into a furry ball, weight against her chest, and began to purr.

Kat's dreams were bad before, but never like this one. She felt, but couldn't see, someone in her bedroom, ready to hurt her. She shivered and cuddled Black Cat, her greatest consolation when the terrors of the night came. And, yes, they did come.

An owl, close, hooted.

The ancient omen of death.

"Stop it!" Kat told herself. "It is dark, and the bird is on the hunt."

Kat shivered again, and dragged her old, tattered quilt to her neck, just as she had done at 12, after watching the Bela Lugosi version of *Dracula.*

For many dark nights, she believed Dracula would kill her. The quilt comforted her then, just as it did now. It had been a gift of love from Grandmamma Tovslosky. And, though she'd tell no one, she still believed it protected her.

She drifted into a much-needed sleep, smiling in memory of those wonderful days which ended all too soon with the passing of Gran.

Her cell phone played Pachelbel's Canon in D. She hated ringing phones—classical music, even in the tinny-tone played by a cell phone, was better than the horrid ring.

"'O," Kat croaked.

BC, awakened by the noise, jumped in disgust from the bed, the warm indent still where he comforted Kat to sleep.

"Kat, thank God, you're okay!"

"Why wouldn't I be? The closest thing to danger is the phone waking me up with the start I just had!" she stated irritably.

"There's been another one."

"Another what—" The import of Bart's words connected. The fog in her brain shot away. "Another murder? Please tell me there hasn't been another murder."

Bart's confident baritone seemed strangely shaky. "Another murder."

"Where?"

"Top of Ravens Ravine, same as the other. This time it's one of our own, more or less."

"Who?"

"I believe it's Miguel Salisto, or what's left of him." Bart still considered Miggie—never known for being an involved town member—a part of Ravens Cove and under his protection.

The safekeeping of this town and its people is my primary duty. And I have failed. Just like I failed the Pantino family. . .

Bart thought back five years ago when he took the job. Although young, he spent a couple of years with the Alaska Troopers and felt ready to take on the challenge of being the lone police officer in a small town.

Until the phone call. A day burned into his memory.

Richard Pantino called to report his wife, Dana, and children missing. The whole town went out to search; the Alaska State Troopers were called in. No sign of them.

Bart spent every day looking for clues to find the family. He prayed to God to bring them back—alive. *It's the last time I asked God for anything.*

Two weeks later, the Troopers found the family in shallow graves ten miles south of Ravens Cove. The children assaulted; the mother, too. Bart still saw the decaying bodies full of maggots and flies.

Richard Pantino grew hateful and locked himself away. When he ventured out, he never missed an opportunity to remind Bart they died because Bart did not find them in time.

A year later, Richard Pantino blew his head off with a sawed-off shot gun.

I failed him, too. . .

"Miggie? Are you sure?" Kat asked.

Kat's question brought Bart back to the present. "Yes."

"Wow. I didn't think his business, or his lifestyle were dangerous. I never understood how Miggie stayed in business. In fact, I never understood why the Congregational Alliance made Miggie a member in good standing. Even in my limited knowledge of Christianity, I always thought it weird. Still, dangerous?"

"I'm not sure his business is connected to his demise," Bart answered.

"Maybe not. What can I do?"

"I need you to be at the office today. The feathers are going to hit the fan when this gets out, and you know it will. Can you be ready in an hour? I'll come get you."

Kat didn't argue. She did not want to cross paths with the killer and be victim number three.

"I'll be ready. PLEASE bring coffee. No food. I don't think my stomach can handle it."

"Will do." Bart hung up.

The wheels of the old, faded, red pickup crunched the gravel, announcing Bart's arrival.

Kat hopped off the porch and met him halfway.

The rich aroma of dark chocolate and coffee struck her nose when she opened the passenger door.

"A mocha! Yum!" Kat rewarded Bart with a thankful smile.

71

They traveled the short distance to town without saying a word. They pulled up in front of the sheriff's office—an empty Main Street greeted them.

Kat breathed a sigh of relief. "Guess no one has heard."

"Probably won't last, but I'll take the quiet for now." Bart rounded the truck and opened the passenger door.

Kat jumped down.

She unlocked the stationhouse door and threw her coat and keys on the desk. "Who found him?"

"Amos Thralling."

"Again?" Kat said in disbelief.

"Yep. I'm going to have to bring Amos in for questioning. I'm not convinced he has anything to do with the murders. All the same, I can't let my feelings run this investigation—would you track him down?"

Kat glanced at her watch. "He's fishing by now."

"Don't know why he thinks he can fish at this time of year, but just like the sun, Amos rises every morning and goes out for the big one," Bart answered.

"Always has."

"See what you can do to find him, just the same?"

"I'll call his brother. Get him to track down Amos and bring him to the station."

"Thanks. I'm going to the ravine to take a look at Miggie before he's shipped to Anchorage. Man, the FBI guy will be much harder to get rid of after this."

Shaking his head, Bart turned on his left foot, and strode to his office to grab his hat. He breezed past Kat, out into a grey, gloomy day. The mountains hid behind a blanket of low-lying, moisture-filled clouds.

Any forensic evidence will be destroyed if it snows, or worse rains, on Miggie's corpse before I can get there. Bart pushed the old red truck's accelerator to the floor.

Yesterday's crime scene tape greeted him. Miggie occupied the exact spot and lay in the exact same position as John Doe.

"You sicko," Bart said to the unknown perpetrator. "I'll get you, whoever you are."

Something rustled from the direction of the path.

Bart drew his gun, pointing it down the ravine. "You hiding in there, show yourself right now!"

"Whatcha doing?"

Bart jumped a few inches to his left, swung around and pointed the gun at Ken Melbourne.

Unshaken, Ken crouched down and studied the path leading to the dark opening of the ravine. "Full daylight, gloomy day though it is, and not an ounce of light shining into the chasm?" Ken shot a questioning look at Bart.

Ignoring the implied request for information, Bart lowered his gun, holstering it with a snap. "What on earth are you doing here, Melbourne?"

"I came up to look at yesterday's crime scene. Odd to see a corpse. I'm sure yesterday's is under autopsy in Anchorage."

Bart's shoulders sagged under the shame he felt from the inability to protect the people of Ravens Cove. "This would be one of ours. Same place, same position, same everything."

"May I take a look?"

Bart gestured with his head towards Miggie Salisto's corpse.

Ken walked over, looking as he went, ensuring he didn't contaminate any potential evidence.

The lurch in his stomach shocked him. He saw all types of murders in his career. Both at the crime scene and in pictures. Human teeth marks so perfect and so deep in flesh, they could cast a mold and arrest the perpetrator once caught. He witnessed firsthand his share of the horror men could do to each other. The scene in front of him surpassed all of them.

The stench reminded him of a monthlong, decomposed drowning victim. The skinless corpse's muscle liquified at a rapid rate, dropping a thick, pungent fluid onto the ground. As quickly as the red, stinking globules hit the ground, the land absorbed it, leaving the area stained but dry.

Ken leaned closer. "There are no eyes!"

The sockets drained a black and purple fluid. In fact, most of the stench came from the eye sockets.

Ken straightened and turned a wan face toward the sheriff. "In all my time, I've never seen any chemical or poison to cause this."

Bart shot a surprised look to Ken. He never heard a suit guy admit not knowing everything. If they didn't know, they tried to sound like they did.

"I've already ascertained as much. So, then, is there any reason for you to be here, Agent Melbourne?"

"Sometimes, Sheriff, it takes two to make sense of something. I believe we should combine our knowledge and get moving on solving this before there's another victim. Serial killers have patterns, and this pattern is frightening."

Ken turned back to look at the body. He tilted his head up in Bart's direction. "I'd expect another murder tonight. There won't be much left of this town, in very short order, if we don't stop the perp soon."

Bart pondered this. Whether he liked it or not, this suit made a good point.

"Tell you what, Melbourne, you can follow along. But if you try to take over, if you even think about giving orders to anyone, you'll be out of here."

Small victory, but victory just the same, Ken thought.

"Agreed." He held out his hand.

This time the Sheriff took it.

Bart and Ken scoured the area, hoping to find even a tiny shred of a clue. No luck.

The medical team arrived to take Miggie Salisto's remains to the funeral home, the closest thing to a morgue in Ravens Cove, to await dispatch to the medical examiner in Anchorage.

CHAPTER 12

A SUSPECT SURFACES

"No, Mrs. Tellamoot, this is *not* a ghost," Kat stated. *The old legends of Ravens Ravine are being stirred up like a long-silent bees' nest getting bumped in the spring.*

"It's the legend! It has come to life!"

"This is not a legend, Mrs. Tellamoot, these are homicides!"

"Killings just like the legend, Katrina—the legend handed down! This thing is back."

"These are murders, Mrs. Tellamoot. Don't believe this is supernatural. So lock your doors, and make sure Benny is on guard."

"Benny doesn't do much more than bark these days," Mrs. Tellamoot said of her half wolf–half husky.

"At least he could warn you. If Benny barks, you call here or my cell, okay?"

"Yes." Mrs. Tellamoot sounded somewhat relieved as they hung up.

The door chimed just as Kat returned the phone to its cradle.

Bart and Agent Melbourne walked in. They obviously reached some sort of truce earlier, but the suspension of hostilities didn't explain Bart acting like he just found his long, lost friend.

"Bart?"

"Mornin', Kat. Thanks again for coming in. How's it going?" Bart asked.

Kat watched he and Ken continue toward Bart's office, deep in conversation.

Mr. Smooth stopped in his tracks, as if he'd just been snapped out of a trance, looked back, and said, "Good morning, Kat."

The ire rose. "You have no invitation to call me by the name reserved for my closest friends and family! It's Ms. Tovslosky to you, Agent Melbourne." Kat turned to her report and began to type, fast.

Ken smiled. 'She's a looker,' his Uncle Ed would have said. Dark hair, green eyes, small upturned nose. Appeared somewhat Irish and yet not. Whatever the genes, they had come together to make her someone hard to ignore. He decided to call her Kat anyway. It fit. On the ready, claws out, one warning-swipe accompanied by a growl. This could get to be fun. *I wonder how angry she'll get?*

Ken resumed the conversation with Bart. Who, to his surprise, possessed more knowledge than Ken first thought. In fact, Bart was a bright man and well-studied. Made it somewhat understandable as to why he resisted any help. His stubbornness struck a deep chord in Ken. *It's like studying my own reflection.*

Bart stopped at his doorway. "Did they find Amos yet?"

"Nope. But Arnie did say they would get here as soon as he could track him down."

"Interrupt me for Amos or a call from the Anchorage ME."

Bart and Ken entered Bart's office. Kat could hear murmuring and hushed sounds as they worked to piece the puzzle together.

Kat prayed they could. A dead John Doe made it scary. A dead member of Ravens Cove made it personal, then terrifying.

"God help us." Kat did not make a habit of praying, but she thought a small plea couldn't hurt.

The ME's office called at the same time Amos and Arnie sidled through the door.

"When it rains, it pours."

"What?" Arnie Thralling asked.

"Sorry, talking to myself today. I'll be right with you."

"Do you need me for anything? I've got a boat to overhaul and winterize."

"No, just Amos. Thanks for finding him for us, Arnie." She graced him with a dazzling smile.

Arnie relaxed, hung his head, and grinned like a schoolboy. "Welcome, Miss."

Kat put the ME's call through to Bart and escorted Amos to the coffee room, which doubled as their interrogation room.

"How's the fishing?"

"No luck. But there's always tomorrow. I sure won't have any luck later today when I'm done here, thanks to Sheriff Bart wantin' to talk."

"I know. But you have discovered two bodies in two days. Don't you think they might be a little more important than fishing?"

Amos wrinkled his brow in thought.

The gesture said it all about Amos and about most of the town's residents. Nothing took precedence over fishing.

"Guess so," he said, half meaning it.

"Make yourself comfy, Amos." Kat offered him a cup of black coffee, packets of fake cream and real sugar, and a red stir stick.

Amos relaxed. "Thanks."

Kat smiled and left to tackle the all-elusive report.

CHAPTER 13

AN ANGEL SPEAKS

Josiah walked toward the small church at the end of Main as fast as his aged body would allow. He passed the adult shop. Late morning yet the place stood silent. The lights were off. The lack of activity spoke volumes.

Josiah's morning prayers confirmed his feeling about another death. He knew someone connected with Ravens Cove to be the victim. His heart grew heavy. The owner of this place had welcomed evil into his life. Josiah knew an eternal soul had again been lost to the Evil One.

"So many, O God, so many!" Anger, then urgency, replaced sadness.

The Thing, all he could call it, as he did not know its name, grew stronger at an even faster rate than he first suspected. *It must be drawing strength from a source in addition to the victims.*

As if to confirm this, the Congregational Alliance building drew his attention. He chose to walk on the opposite side of the street to get a better view of the black being guarding the door.

What a beautiful building to accommodate such evil.

Uriel, the angel who accompanied Josiah on his journeys, spoke. "Look with your mind's eye, Josiah. Why would such evil be at home in a building of worship?"

Understanding dawned. Josiah realized this church, and what went on behind its closed doors, strengthened the Thing. Just like all evil beings, adoration gave it as much, if not more, power than the violence it so craved.

"Pride goeth before the fall, dark one, pride before the fall!" He whispered the well-known verse of Proverbs to the dark being covering the door.

Atramentous shivered as if a cold breeze touched his black core. He turned blood red eyes on Josiah.

"You do not fear me, evil one. And it is not you I fear. I fear the One who is true and just. Fear Him! In the mighty name of Jesus Christ!" Josiah's voice rose and caught the attention of a passerby.

The woman stopped in her tracks. She crossed to the sidewalk in front of the Congregational Alliance, walking through the invisible tail of the mist.

Atramentous strengthened when he encountered the passerby's fear.

"The deceit is endless, O God. How are we to know?" Josiah lamented.

Atramentous refocused his attention on Josiah. A long, fog of an arm shot out and toward Josiah.

Uriel stepped in front of Josiah, raising a golden sword toward the appendage. "He is not yours!"

Atramentous glared at the angel. "You have the advantage—this time. But we have plans for that man. And once we have the souls Iconoclast needs, you won't stop us!"

Atramentous's semi-transparent limb snaked back to his body. "Enjoy your small victory for now; we will win this war."

CHAPTER 14

A BETTER SUSPECT

Paul Lucas fell to his knees in prayer when he heard of Miggie Salisto's death. "I never condoned Miggie's business. But, O God, I agonized over the eternal fate awaiting him. Now it is too late. And I grieve for another one lost to deceit.

"Why do you allow the Congregational Alliance to exist? It approves of its members practicing the black arts and peddling pornography which is directly against your teachings. How, O God, can you let it continue?"

The door opened and Paul turned. His heart sank.

"We must talk, Pastor Lucas."

Paul examined the deep lines creasing Josiah's face. Shock flooded Paul. The deep contours evidenced a burden on this man Paul missed— no ignored—the day before.

"Forgive me, Lord." Paul whispered. "What can I do for you, Mr. . . .?"

"Josiah Williams," he hurried on, "please hear me out before you cast me from your church as a crazy old man. I have not always been the way I am now."

Paul motioned for Josiah to sit beside him on one of the folding chairs, serving as pews for his church.

"First, I am a believer in the Lord Jesus Christ. I did not believe until a few years ago. I lived what I thought to be a wonderful life, complete with a beautiful wife and two beautiful children. I did not spend much time at home. I traveled for work, and when in town I patronized the local bar, most nights until it closed. My friends were my drinking buddies."

"Where is your family, now, Mr. Williams? Why are you in Ravens Cove without them?"

"They are dead, Pastor. Have been for over ten years. And it is my fault."

Alarm bells sounded in Paul's head. *Is this the murderer making a confession?* He prayed for guidance and help.

"How is it your fault, Josiah?" Paul placed a shaky hand over the man's brown, wrinkled one.

"I did not protect them. They were murdered while I whooped it up at my favorite bar. You see, a great evil took over my town. A place not much bigger than Ravens Cove. They were victims of said evil. In my wife's most dire time, I failed her. Can you imagine her terror and heartbreak in those final moments?"

"I can. I do."

"If I were there, I might have stopped it. They might still be alive. I killed them, sure as life."

Relief flooded Paul. *Guilt-ridden and a little off, maybe, but not a serial killer. Grief can drive a person to the brink of insanity. I've seen it many times.*

"My heart breaks for you. And I am amazed you are a believer now after such a horror happening in your life. Many run from God at those times, yet you turned to Him. Why?"

"Mostly by God's intervention. In addition, I have an ability to see things, things no one else can. So, once I was ready to accept Jesus as my Lord, it was an easy leap to believe in what others do not see. Do you understand?"

"No."

"As a child, I played with imaginary friends. As I grew older, these specters did not leave, and I realized no one else could see them. Then, the dreams came. Dreams and visions which came true. I tried to talk to my parents. They threatened me with a mental hospital. I learned to be quiet to avoid being labeled as a crazy."

No kidding, thought Paul. He knew at times it took great effort to just listen and not judge. *Abba Father, help me to help this man.*

Josiah stopped talking and searched Paul's eyes. "Thank you for trying to be open, Pastor Lucas. This is hard for anyone to understand, most of all me."

Paul said nothing.

Josiah continued, "The older I got the more I turned to anything to make these visions leave. I tried drugs as a teenager, but they made the images worse. I started to sneak alcohol and found some relief. So, I hid in the bottle more and more. And in my cups is where I could be found on the night The Thing murdered my family and most of my town."

"The Thing?"

"I don't have a name for it. But it is a strong servant of the Evil Foe. From what I've discovered, it moves around the earth. After destroying one town, it goes on to another of its appointed places.

"Ten years ago, a believing minister and his congregation threw it out of my small town. The tide turned in the battle when several people of the town chose to believe the minister and joined him in the battle. I believed the nightmare to be over." Josiah wiped his forehead with a handkerchief.

"Please go on," Paul said.

"Five years ago, it destroyed a small town in China. The Chinese government attributed it to a mining accident. Since such accidents are common in China, it made for good cover. But the odd thing is these 'miners,' which included women and children, all died within a five-day period. And though the government said they weren't found for days—its explanation for the extreme decomposition of the bodies—a family member reportedly spoke with one of the victims a day before the discovery. I realized I made a mistake by believing this thing to be destroyed.

"I could not go to China, but I still saw the destruction taking place in my dreams and morning prayers. This is a horrible affliction! Our God knows why I have the gift of dreams and visions."

"So, you think this thing is here? Why here, Mr. Williams?" Paul asked.

"I don't have the answer, Pastor. I didn't even know why I felt compelled to come to Ravens Cove until I arrived. I have dreamed of this place. I have seen your church in my sleep. And I felt the dread I experienced before.

"I could not stay away, and now I will not leave. I can't stand by knowing what will happen as The Thing works in secret to destroy Ravens Cove. I must try to help!" Josiah's voice rose well above its natural calm.

Alarmed, and in an attempt to placate the hysteria Paul thought he perceived, he again placed a hand on Josiah's. "What can I do to help you find peace?"

"This evil one will not stop until it destroys every person in Ravens Cove. Its mission is to murder believers, at the hand of unbelievers, and take as many souls as possible before they can reach the Lord."

Josiahpaused. The blackened door of the Congregational Alliance swam into his mind's eye.

"Ravens Cove is ripe for the picking, Pastor. There is a wickedness here, and it's been a festering boil in this town for many years.

"I say this because there is a black spirit covering the Congregational Alliance and—for all its outward piety— it is a magnet, a draw of power for this entity. Otherwise, the black mist would not be there."

Paul weighed the plausibility of Josiah's statement. It would explain the loathing spewed at him from, and on behalf of, Martin Plotno since the day Paul arrived in Ravens Cove.

Paul remembered praying and praying for reconciliation, and to be shown his sin which caused such a—he did not want to even think it—hatred toward him. His lamented at how his small church lost more than a few people because of the lies perpetrated by the parishioners and the head of the Congregational Alliance.

"I can allow that Plotno is misguided. But evil? That's a harsh word."

"I know this is hard to believe, Pastor. I know. I have seen the destruction firsthand and still must pray to believe what cannot be proved by cold, hard facts. I would much rather forget it and move on with my life. But I cannot.

"Since I arrived, I have seen the signs pointing to The Thing being here. If you are unable to believe there is an malevolent being protecting The Congregational Alliance, then the first victim may convince you.

"This Thing sucks the soul and blood from its victims. The body shows signs of advanced decay. The bones are pulp, the eye sockets are empty. There is no skin. The muscles are red but mushy. The stench is one of a corpse long dead." Josiah took a breath.

"There is one unmistakable sign confirming these are not murders at human hands, and it is The Thing we are up against. Once the eyes are cleared, as will be done in an autopsy, there will be a pinprick through the back of each socket. The brains of the victim were sucked out through those pricks. There is nothing left."

Paul felt he made a hasty decision on this man's innocence. If this turned out to be true, this man must be involved. "How would I back up these facts, Mr. Williams?"

"Go to the sheriff; tell him what I have said. He can confirm the state of the corpse."

"Why don't you go to the sheriff, Mr. Williams?" Paul knew the answer. Josiah would be arrested on the spot. If not convicted of the murders, he'd surely be sent to the closest psych ward.

Josiah rose to leave. "He will hear you better than me. We'll speak soon."

Paul did not look forward to another of these conversations. He did, however, look forward to talking to Bart Andersen.

Josiah all but gave him permission to relate their conversation to the sheriff, and he would. As soon as he felt enough time passed, Paul jogged to the station.

The bell swung in a wild back and forth motion from the force of Paul's entrance.

Kat jumped at the noise.

The phones and steady questions from the townspeople having all but stopped, she could, for once, focus on the second paragraph of the report on Miggie. Her shoulders slumped at the frustration she felt once again.

Kat straightened and turned toward the counter. Pastor Paul Lucas, white as a sheet and out of breath, stood silent.

He has to be one of the politest people in Ravens Cove, contrary to all the rumors, Kat thought.

"Hi, Paul. What brings you here today?"

"Need to see Bart," Paul said in between gasps for breath.

"Busy. Second body in two days."

"I believe I have information about the murders, Ms. Tovslosky."

Kat looked at him. "I'll get the Sheriff. Sit down and catch your breath. Want some water?"

"Thank you. Water would be great."

Sheriff Bart had closed his normally open door in an effort to ward off any visitors or unnecessary phone calls.

Kat knocked. No answer. Kat cracked the door and looked at Bart. She heard him saying, "Sulfur is a main component in the goo coming out the eyes ..."

Kat did a fake-cough. Bart stopped, raised his head and glared. "What is it?"

Kat ignored the angry tone. "Pastor Lucas is here. Says he has information about the case. Where do you want him?

"Amos still occupies the coffee/interview room. He's writing out a statement of what he saw, and anything he could think of to clear him of being the prime suspect."

"Guess he realized solving these murders took precedence over his fishing routine, especially when I said, 'You are a 'person of interest,'" Bart answered.

"Seems so. Now, where do I put Pastor Lucas?"

"Give me a minute to get ready, and then bring him in here."

Kat ushered Paul in, the door whispered to a close behind him. She glanced quickly through the glass pane.

Whatever Paul said made Bart study the medical examiner's report. He looked back at Paul. Fifteen minutes later, Bart and Ken thanked Paul and followed him out the door.

Bart hesitated and turned around. "Back in a bit. Tell Amos he can leave when his statement is complete. Think we have a better suspect."

"A better suspect? Do I know . . ." The bell chimed and the door closed, leaving her in midsentence.

"Where do you think we can find this Josiah Williams?" Ken asked.

"Well, as there is just one place to stay in town, I think we'll start there. If we don't find him there, we'll find him soon enough. Gotta love a small town. The man can't get far without someone seeing him and happily sharing his whereabouts."

Ken smiled. Any upside to this place would do. If you counted the beautiful Ms. Tovslosky, and he did, then there were two upsides to Ravens Cove.

CHAPTER 15

SECRETS

Anita burst through Atramentous and the door he covered. She felt a chill and took it for excitement over the man of her dreams. She rushed up to Plotno, fell in his arms, and sobbed.

"Did you hear?" she asked.

"Indeed, one of our brothers is gone. He has been taken from us and in such a horrible way. A martyr for our god."

Anita wiped the forced tears, but lingered against his strong, firm chest. She pulled back and looked up into Plotno's flint-colored eyes. "He will be missed. Even if he did run such an odd little business."

"To each his own, Anita, to each his own. Our god uses all for his purpose. We are not to judge. Just to love."

Anita's heartbeat quickened from the adoration she felt for this accepting, wonderful man. "You're right as always. I'll be happy to plan the funeral. So many would want to say goodbye."

"Under the circumstances, I believe a memorial service would be better. I don't think there is much left to be viewed."

"True. I'll call Starr and Autumn to help."

"You're such an asset." Plotno touched the curve of Anita's cheek and smiled into her eyes. "Thank you."

In a silent but clear dismissal, Plotno turned back to the sermon he had already written and been practicing for the memorial. *This must be a pep talk for the congregation to see how special and right they are. One of their own sacrificed because of their goodness.*

He smiled and took a moment to bask in his talent to both write and persuade. *Important*, he though, *when a leader must whip up his followers to do an evil deed in the name of God.*

Anita watched her beloved at work. He exuded strength and power. And he would be hers. She thanked her god Miggie died after her visit. She could never have gotten what she needed to cast her spell of love and bondage on this man.

She headed for the door and shot through Atramentous again.

Still stinging from losing his reward of Miggie, he lashed out and punched Anita between the shoulder blades.

"Oomph." Anita lurched forward.

Her guardian, Venenose, distracted by the boring task of watching this creature, so happily and unsuspectingly going to her doom, snapped out of his mental haze. He shot forward and caught Anita before she tumbled, headfirst, down the concrete stairs.

Atramentous giggled the laugh of a small, mischievous child.

Iconoclast had reminded Venenose of this woman's import just minutes before.

"If you fail to protect this mortal, I will cast you into the abyss for eternity."

Venenose glared into Atramentous' dead, black pools, and bared his red carnivore's teeth. "You'll pay, you dumb lout. You almost cost me my freedom, and I won't forget it."

Atramentous hissed in reply but did nothing. He knew, but would never admit, Venenose's strength to be superior to his own. He believed if Venenose ever got the chance, he would not hesitate to exact revenge.

Anita looked back to the church door. She felt a push right before she tripped. Just like when her little brother shoved her from behind, and she did not hear him coming. She shivered and took each step with care, gripping the railing until she reached bottom.

At the sidewalk, she made a hard right turn, almost running into Artie Thralling. She leveled disdainful and accusatory eyes on him.

"Excuse me," Artie mumbled.

Anita broke eye contact and quickened her step toward her home and goal. *I have two hours before I'm missed at work.* She smiled. *Plenty of time to begin the spell.*

She unlocked the door of her small wood house. The white lace curtains in the windows, the blue-green door and the grey siding presented a beautiful, well-kept home which said, "warmth." The exterior contradicted the dark arts practiced within.

Anita stepped through the front door, Venenose her shadow, and hurried to the basement to begin preparations. She thrilled to the thought of consummating her love, impatient to begin her new life with Martin Plotno.

"Soon, my love, soon. Your wife doesn't stand a chance!"

Venenose sneered at her naiveté. "You'll definitely end up in the same place as Plotno—after the demon feast."

Like Atramentous, he awaited the day he could eat his fill of her fear and terror. The anticipation brought a malevolent smile to his lips, revealing sharp, bloodstained teeth.

It has been so long since the last banquet of flesh and bone and souls. Commander Iconoclast has already had his fill of two!

Venenose comforted himself knowing he would be first to eat, after Iconoclast, because of his rank. His blackness increased in size at the pride of his name, Fatal, given him by the great Evil Foe. He snatched many souls from the One who created these horrible mortals in the first place.

He shrank in fear at the idea he would one day face the One who died, yet lived. The One who had power over death and Hades. He could not say the name; it would destroy him.

Venenose knew the truth. He witnessed God's glory before he joined the great rebellion to ultimately be thrown from heaven in shame.

Venenose's focus snapped back to the present. *This stupid mortal is getting ready to destroy the whole spell! I must do everything; thus, I deserve to eat this human soon. When I do, I will take my time and relish her pain and fear.*

Anita worked at a fevered pace, impatient to begin her life with Plotno.

"Stop," he roared into Anita's mind.

She became a human statue.

"You are doing it all wrong. Read!" The hatred and loathing shot out before he could stop it. He fought for control. When he spoke again, he used a sickening-sweet tone which made him want to throw up—if he could throw up.

"Read the book; look at the spells, Anita; you are doing it all wrong. You want the man; you need the man; you can't live without him. So slow down and take note."

Anita relaxed. She didn't recognize the first voice, but the second contained her guardian's gentle whisper. She felt safe now. She stopped and reviewed the instructions and realized she almost made a terrible mistake. She would have murdered her beloved instead of capturing his heart. *These things are tricky.*

"Thank you, Guardian," she whispered.

Anita focused all her attention on the concoction, measuring and chanting the words with care. *It must simmer for a while, twenty-four hours to be exact, untouched, in darkness.*

She looked at her watch, sighed and snatched her purse off the rough-hewn table. She checked her hair in the brass mirror. She gave a sharp nod of approval to her reflection. *Time to return to my character of librarian.*

"How I long for the day I can reveal my true self, the powerful witch, so all will fear me!"

Anita glanced one last time at the small kettle, rounded at the bottom, a combination kettle and pressure cooker, beginning to simmer on the stove. She smiled.

"Tomorrow a new day and new love awaits!" She ran up the basement stairs, grabbed her coat and whisked out the door.

Venenose stayed behind to monitor the brew. If it burned, the deceit would not be complete, and the plan could fail.

"What a dolt! Believing this is a spell. So easy to fool most of these people.

"The truth is so much more logical. Iconoclast's many minions are fanning the lust in Plotno to a point where he can't resist this woman.

Profligacy just entered Plotno. And he is only one of the many who live inside the pastor and masquerade as his idea of God. Destruction is close now!" Venenose felt pleased with the plan's progress, very pleased indeed.

CHAPTER 16

TRUTHS

Kat watched Bart and Ken escort Josiah into the office. She shivered. *This man knows my name, and he may be the killer!*

Bart led Josiah into the coffee room, but purposely didn't offer him anything to drink. *Better make him as uncomfortable as possible from the start.*

"Mr. Williams, can you tell me what brings you to our small town … at an odd time of year, I might add?" Bart asked.

"Business."

The cryptic and calm reply did not answer the question.

"What kind of business, Mr. Williams?"

Here we go. Josiah braced himself for the ridicule, the look stating, "Crazy as a loon." *Well, I can only blame myself. I talked to Paul Lucas to both enlist his help and in hopes he would bring me to the attention of the sheriff. It worked.*

Josiah let out a sigh. "God's business."

The crazy-as-my-Aunt-Millie look settled over Bart's eyes. Bart's eyebrows raised. "God's business? Please explain to us," he motioned to include Ken, "what is so important in the isolated and small town of Ravens Cove to cause God to send you here?"

Josiah looked to the man leaning against the wall at the front of the room semi guarding the door and analyzing Josiah's every move.

Not as much disbelief from the *Sheriff as there is in this one,* Josiah noted.

Ken continued to study Josiah. He doubted the quiet, unassuming, not to mention old, man before him could be capable of committing these horrific and gory killings.

Still, the superhuman strength some murderers possessed amazed him. He remembered one case in which a 5-foot, 100-pound woman, lugged a corpse to the edge of a cliff and rolled it down. She had been a bodybuilder. Her strength doubled by adrenaline. When it came to getting rid of a body, people could accomplish Herculean feats, impossible under normal circumstances.

But, how did he speed up the rate of decomposition?

Ken straightened. "Yes, we'd be interested to know why God would send you here," he said.

"I don't ask questions, sir. I go where the Lord directs."

This is like pulling a king salmon from the river right as it comes in from the ocean, Bart thought. *Maybe we will get more if Ken and I team up. At least shake him up a little.*

Bart motioned Ken to join them at the table.

Ken strode forward and stood across from Josiah.

"It has come to my attention, Mr. Williams, you have much knowledge about the murders occurring in this small town."

Yes, Paul came to see the Sheriff. This is good.

"Yes, I do."

"Then, you can see why you have become a person of interest, and in all honesty, our main suspect in this investigation?"

"Yes."

"OK. Please explain why you have detailed knowledge of the murders, when even the newspapers have not reported on some of the facts you shared with Pastor Lucas."

Josiah sighed, then prayed, *Lord, guide me. Give me words to convince these people of my truthfulness. In your name Jesus, I pray for truth now. Amen.*

"I have seen this before, in my own town, ten years back. I researched it and found the same thing which happened in my town happened in China five years ago. Those details were harder to confirm because the Chinese government did its best to keep the facts out of the world press.

"God did instruct me, through much prayer and meditation, to come to Ravens Cove. I did not know why until I arrived."

Bart and Ken turned cold, unbelieving eyes to Josiah.

How many times, O God, must I relive the horror of losing my family? How many times must I share these most intimate and painful memories with strangers?

Josiah fought back the tears. In a strangled voice, he continued, "I'm sure Pastor Lucas told you my story, as much as I shared with him anyway."

"I'd like to hear it from you," Bart answered.

"As I told Pastor Lucas, my family, along with 90 percent of my hometown, became murder victims. What I did not tell the Pastor is some of the deaths were attributed to others in the community; people who were never violent in their lives.

"The initial deaths were just as you have seen with your first two victims. The deaths at the hands of the townspeople came after.

"The odd thing, though, no matter how the person died, the deaths had one common thread—A pinpoint hole in each eye socket, and the brains were gone. Even if they were shot, hatcheted, bludgeoned or remained intact otherwise, they had no brains.

"The police allowed me to look at the crime scene photographs. The first time they hoped to shock me into a confession. The second at my request after I'd been cleared of charges.

"My babies' brains were missing; my beautiful wife's robin's-egg blue eyes were missing. But neither my wife nor my children had purple and black seeping from their eye sockets. And she and the babies were found, each baby curled against her as if sleeping. No horror on their faces; in fact, I saw a peace I never understood." Josiah dropped his eyes, studying the fine lines on the back of his hands, willing away the tears.

Bart cleared his throat.

"I apologize. I'll continue."

"I have not seen these bodies firsthand in Ravens Cove. But I could not help but overhear the townspeople gathered on Main Street when I came into town. Parts of those conversations confirmed my assumptions."

"Maybe I could believe this," Ken replied, "if you reported only what you heard through the rumor mill. But you have information only the killer knows."

Kat leaned toward the coffee room in hopes of overhearing the conversation. *Darn! Can't hear a thing.*

She grabbed Arnie's incident report and walked to the copier just outside of the room.

"Agent Melbourne, I am not a murderer. Well, I am one by neglect. I should have been protecting my family against the evil which overtook my home. Instead I drank with my buddies while the mayor of our small town obtained entry into my home and proceeded to shoot my wife and two children and then turn the gun on himself."

"Likely story," Kat muttered, and then threw her hand over her mouth, hoping Bart did not hear her.

Josiah, knowing Kat could hear him, and hoping he could touch her spirit with his words, continued, "If this is what I believe it is, there will be at least two more deaths. One tonight and another the night after."

"Not on my watch!" Bart said.

Josiah turned patient and unbelieving eyes to Bart. "I'm afraid so, Sheriff. You can't control this. It is not a man doing these killings. At least not yet. This is the work of a spirit.

"It has various places it claims as its dominion on this earth. If anything has been built on its 'home,' as it were, during its time away, then it becomes a feeding ground. If not, he checks all his various domains until he finds a feeding ground.

"From what I can tell, going back through as much history as I have, this entity and others like it claimed many areas on this earth. It visited Ravens Cove at a time coinciding with Captain Cook's voyage to Alaska in 1778. If I'm not mistaken, there is a legend confirming this."

"Don't start on the old myth, Mr. Williams! Every time something unexplainable occurs in Ravens Cove, the legend is blamed. It is a local tale, a story to stop children from wandering too far from their homes. Nothing more!"

"Not true," Josiah answered.

Bart leaned forward, a red tint rising up his neck to his cheeks. "How dare you . . ."

Josiah held up his hand. "I will speak of it no more for now."

Bart relaxed.

Josiah continued, "As I said, this thing has numerous areas on this earth it considers home. And Ravens Cove, although uninhabited land for many years, is now settled and thus a prime hunting ground.

"There is much going on which invited this thing to stay and destroy. There are members of your community who worship it and its type. Their flagrant hatred contradicts all God considers good and is the bait, for lack of a better term. Their acts grow more brazen every day. At the right time, these people, these ones you have known well and accepted as family in this town, will turn on you. They will do all they can to destroy the true believers and then burn the town to the ground."

"If what you say is true, then this Thing is not logical at all," said Ken. "Ravens Cove is tiny. I could see it somewhere like, say, New York, where the population is staggering."

"It has assigned dwelling places. It has no authority anywhere else. So, it destroys all it can when it can. And as it destroys, it grows stronger. There is enough here to satisfy its quest for power and authority. One soul is a great loss to God. It relishes this prize above all else."

"Are you trying to tell us the Devil is here in Ravens Cove? Because if you are, Mr. Williams, please note you are on shaky ground! I've had about enough of these crazy ramblings!"

"Not the Devil, but one of his most valued servants. One who grew more powerful over the centuries from destroying out-of-the-way, unknown towns and villages. One who knows how to stay under the radar, as it were. Evil works in secret; once exposed to the light of truth it loses its power."

"Well, I'm going to take this opportunity to exercise *my* power, Mr. Williams. I believe you have given me enough probable cause to keep you here for at least twenty-four hours. And I'm going to do just that. This trumped up story—which is what it is sir—has just won you a free night in the town jail. And, even if I wouldn't have held you before, the threat more will die tonight, makes it my bound duty to keep you here."

Josiah shrugged, then looked Bart in the eye. "Do what you must. It will not stop the murders from occurring. Unless you listen to me, they will happen. As sure as the moon will rise tonight, they will happen."

"Well, I'm doing my part to make sure they don't." Bart motioned Josiah to stand and ushered him to the little-used cell in the back of the station.

Bruit, Iconoclast's lookout, listened to the entire interrogation. He scurried from the room, headed to tell his boss of Josiah's humiliation and incarceration.

Short in height, a more solid form than Atramentous and Venenose, his darkness projected a small shadow as he ran into a sunbeam peeking through the otherwise grey sky. He growled. Light revealed his true form, and it sapped his strength. Winded by the brief encounter, he dove underground.

Kat turned her head. She examined the wall below Bart's office window, looking for the child-size shadow she saw flit past the corner of her eye. Nothing there.

"Great, all the crazy talk has me seeing things." She looked toward the window facing Main to revel in the sunbeam brightening the otherwise dark day.

The inactivity on Main Street disconcerted her. Ravens Cove had been abuzz the last evening. Today, it felt like a blanket of invisible snow fell and insulated the town's normal noises. Footsteps and closing doors seemed muffled. She couldn't hear the birds.

"You okay?" Ken asked.

"Fine, thanks, FBI." She turned back to her copying.

You are one cold fish. How could such a warm and inviting-looking young woman be so full of frost? Sad, he thought, then smiled.

"Don't suppose you'd like to get some dinner later? We could have some fun before I leave for Anchorage."

Kat narrowed her eyes. "Not happening, FBI!"

Ken shrugged and turned his attention to solving the murders. *This legend may be the key, he thought.* Bart snapped shut like a clamshell when Ken asked. He mulled over the possibility Kat might have some answers. He decided against asking. He did not need to court any further rejection from the Ice Queen. Ken headed to the next most logical source—the library.

A cold wind blew in from the north as he stepped into sunshine fighting its way through the low-hanging clouds. It gave no warmth. He yanked his jacket collar up and around his neck to ward off the bitter chill.

The cold emphasized the spooky quiet on Main Street. Ken's survival instinct rose to full alert. He scanned the street, all directions, and saw nothing looking the least bit menacing.

"Get ahold of yourself, man," he muttered.

A passerby looked at him and walked just a little faster.

Great, now I'm talking to myself and scaring the fine citizens of Ravens Cove. Hope my self-conversing doesn't make it to the grapevine. If anything could set a town afire, it's rumor and speculation about a stranger, second only to rumor and speculation on a well-known member of the community.

He arrived at the library, walked up the grey, cold steps. *Not a welcoming exterior.*

Ken's library memories were warm ones. He loved the buildings, large or small; he loved the smell of books and seeing walls and rooms lined with bookshelves. This one, however, felt as cold as a butcher's walk-in refrigerator.

He stepped in and strode to the counter. An acne-plagued teenager squinted at a rather new-looking computer screen. No other customers

98

waited at the counter, but this fact didn't stop the teen from ignoring all of Ken's 6-foot-some-odd structure.

Ken looked at a sign.

"Please ring bell for service. Someone will be with you shortly."

They are kidding, right?

Ken cleared his throat. No response. He drummed on the counter. No response. He rang the bell.

The young man finished typing into the hidden memory box, straightened and turned to Ken.

Unbelievable. This kid would have been tarred and feathered in LA.

"Can I help you?"

"I hope so Mr.?"

"Gary, just Gary."

Ken nodded. "Ok, Gary. Where's the section on Ravens Cove history?"

Gary graced Ken with a blank stare, blinking several times in an effort to return from byte land.

Anytime now, Partner.

"Umm, Ms. Conner, where's the stuff on Ravens Cove?" he asked the empty foyer.

Ken looked around. He and Gary appeared to be the only occupants of the building.

A trim, attractive woman stood up from behind the counter. She held several large periodicals. Scowling at the intruder, she dropped the periodicals on the desk behind the counter and pointed to Ken's left.

"Next room, second aisle from the windows, bottom shelf, but there's not much there. Ravens Cove is a pretty boring little town." She forced a smile at Ken, not covering her irritation at all.

"And your name is?" Ken asked.

"Anita Connor."

"Thank you, Ms. Connor." The salutation came out with as much ease as the smile came over Anita's face.

"Welcome." Anita dropped to the floor behind the counter.

Right where she said it would be. And just as she said, not a wealth of information on the topic of Ravens Cove. Ken wondered if this town existed at all. Maybe, just maybe, he would wake to discover he was in a dream. In just a day, he felt like he jumped down the rabbit hole and entered Alice's Wonderland. He stifled the desire to pinch himself.

Ken stood up and walked back to the counter. He rang the bell without hesitation and started speaking before the teen looked him in the eye. "Not there. Is there anything on legends or myths of Ravens Cove and its surrounding areas?"

Anita popped up. She didn't like the stranger asking this particular question, but she couldn't pinpoint why. *He's attractive and polite, so why is he such an irritation?* "Most of our legends are word of mouth, Mr. ...?"

"Melbourne." He felt an unexplained repulsion at the thought of shaking her hand, so he left his arm at his side. "Is there anyone I could speak to about the legends?"

Anita stood silent for a moment, trying to decide how she could avoid answering. She couldn't.

"Grandma Bricken would be your best choice. She is the expert."

Gary shot an alarmed look sideways to Anita, still pretending to be staring at the screen.

Anita ignored it and hoped this intruder missed it.

He didn't. But never daunted by a challenge, which it sounded like this Grandma Bricken could be, he didn't let on. "Do you know where I can find her?"

"The new church, helping the guy who runs it do whatever he does when he's not pretending to be a pastor." Her venom was palpable.

Feeling he had worn out his dubious welcome, Ken thanked Anita and Gary, turned and headed out to find Grandma Bricken.

"What a yucky man!" Anita said, turning back to the task at hand.

Gary stopped himself before saying, "I thought the guy seemed okay," and instead went back to his typing, knowing better than to challenge Anita and raise her temper.

Her ire knew no bounds, including physical, and he could not afford to take her punishment. He'd learned the hard lesson the first time. And he needed this job or his mom, dad and siblings couldn't survive in Ravens Cove.

Gary typed with focused intent, willing himself to ignore her searching eyes. He let out a silent breath when Anita Connor returned to her task.

CHAPTER 17

THE LEGEND REVEALED

Grandma Bricken hummed happily standing at the stove, cooking being her favorite past time. October meant time to finish canning the cranberries and blueberries collected and frozen during the August harvest. The tundra-like hills surrounding Ravens Cove abounded with the wild, delicious berries.

A pressure cooker rattling on the cooktop made it almost impossible to hear normal household noises. She tilted her head and listened. *Is that a knock? No one knocks in Ravens Cove.*

She sighed, ran her hands down her apron, drying them as she took her time getting to the hallway. She listened again.

"Mrs. Bricken?" Ken called out.

Grandma Bricken stopped at the mirror. Strands of silver, some crow-black mixed in, managed to struggle free from the tight bun atop her head. She smoothed them as much as possible and continued to the door.

Alese Bricken opened the door to a tall, lean, and attractive young man. Even at her age, she appreciated this one. *Movie-star quality,* she thought.

"Mrs. Bricken?"

She stared into the handsome stranger's face. "Who are you?"

"I'm Agent Melbourne." Ken automatically flashed his FBI badge.

"I'm here to assist the sheriff in investigating the recent murders. Your name came up as someone who might be able to clarify a few things. May I come in?"

Grandma Bricken thought this over while looking deep into Ken's eyes, searching him.

Ken had never felt so exposed nor had silence ever been so loud. This woman exuded a personal power he encountered only once or twice in his life. He stood waiting for the decision.

"How did you come to find me?"

Fair question. "Well, I went to the small church down the road," he pointed south, "and the pastor, umm, Lucas I believe, told me where I could find you. This after Anita Conner referred me to you."

Grandma Bricken stepped back from the doorway, allowing enough room for him to enter. She turned her back, walked down the hall and disappeared into a doorway flooding the entry with light.

Ken followed, unsure if he had been invited in or not.

The glorious smells assaulting his senses emanated from the kitchen. A bright, cheery room, in total chaos compared to the rest of the home. There were berries in strainers sitting beside the large, country-style sink—deep and single. Meat sizzled in a large Dutch oven. Potatoes, onions, carrots, and celery stood like a small mountain beside the stove, ready to be added to the meat, he surmised. His stomach growled in response to the smells.

Grandma Bricken's eyebrows lifted.

A small flush rose up Ken's neck. In a flash, he became a small child again, his mother reprimanding him for being underfoot at dinner time. His appetite was insatiable. His growing frame demanded it as a child and still demanded it to keep any weight on him at all.

"What can I do for you, Agent?"

"I'm hoping you will give me some answers about the history of Ravens Cove. It seems there is little written background on this town. And neither Sheriff Bart nor the librarian were helpful in giving me the information I'm looking for. The librarian pointed me in your direction."

If fire could shoot from someone's eyes, it would have from Grandma Bricken's.

"That woman!" She headed to the stove and stirred the aromatic meat with fervor.

She turned back, spoon held high, waving it back and forth. "That woman, if it's what she can be called, sent you to me, sir, because she believes you will not get any answers. And you may not. Her dislike for you, unbeknownst to her, works in your favor.

"She sent you because she knows the legends of my people, who were here before and after the white man set foot in Alaska, are not repeated on a whim. They are not shared with those who would scoff or make a profit from them. My people know these 'legends' and we treat them as a gift of knowledge, not a source of profit or ridicule." She stopped her rampage, eyes wide and wild.

Ken controlled a need to squirm, then run as far as he could from this one. *Eccentric, to say the least. Passionate* would be a more politically correct term; *but I have never been politically correct, so eccentric bordering on batty is my conclusion.*

Ken waited. The spoon hung in midair, pointed at his head. Though it could do no real damage, it would hurt if it hit him. More, he didn't want to arrest this old woman for assaulting a federal agent.

The front door opened, breaking the stare-down.

Ken turned, letting his breath out, thankful for a diversion.

Kat skidded to a halt in the kitchen entry, unhappy to see Ken standing at her grandmother's table.

Okay, two people who scare me. This one may be scarier than Mrs. Bricken, Ken thought.

"What the he... heck are you doing here?"

"Good catch, Katrina. I'd hate to wash your mouth out with soap at your age," Grandma said.

"You wouldn't!" Kat answered.

"I might."

"Fine. Why are you here?"

"I. . . well, the librarian . . . "

"I'll answer for him. As the cat," Grandma chuckled at her pun, "seems to have gotten his tongue."

The play on words did not get lost on Ken, and he felt the embarrassing flush rising up his neck again.

How humiliating! Control yourself, Agent Melbourne, he told himself. Didn't help at all.

Kat didn't seem to notice.

A smile playing on the corners of Mrs. Bricken's mouth said she did. She didn't say anything.

Kat shot a look of challenge to her elder, then thought better of it. She turned her full attention to Ken, her silence demanding an answer.

These two are carbon copies of each other, just decades apart. "You're related?" Ken asked.

"Not because it's any of your business, FBI, but yes."

The Ice Queen's jabs were bad enough. Now her genetic and, most likely, environmental creator, witnessed the ridicule in Kat's tone. The indignation rose. *I'm done!*

Ken turned steady, nonblinking eyes to Kat. "Whether you feel it is or not, Ms. Tovslosky, is of no consequence. Whether you like me being in Ravens Cove or not, I am. These murders are quite the puzzle, and your sheriff has asked me to help." *A little bit of a stretch, but I'm not getting into semantics right now.*

"I want to find the murderer, or murderers, before someone else dies. I need to know the legend everyone is referring to. I may not believe in folklore, but I do believe there are some sick puppies in the world who would grab a story and run with it to get away with murder."

Ken inhaled, then let out a slow, steady breath. *I'm getting loud. Not professional.* This woman brought out the most unprofessional parts of him.

He looked into Kat's eyes. Deep, deep green someone could get lost in. He refocused to the point at hand, forcing his immediate and physical attraction to the background. *This Ice Queen is more trouble than it's worth.*

Kat and her relative both turned matching green eyes on him.

The elder spoke first. "I'm not sure I can help you with what you seek. There is no explanation, at least mortal explanation, for these murders."

"There is always an explanation."

"Yes, but not always a natural one, young man."

Although she sounded crazy to him, when he looked in her eyes, they were sincere and sane.

"Then tell me so I can make some sense of it. We do have a man in custody who may be the murderer, but we need to build a case against him to keep him behind bars."

Grandma Bricken glanced at Kat, asking permission with her eyes. She felt in her heart Kat had deep feelings for this man, albeit unconscious, and she didn't want to risk embarrassing her.

Kat, on the other hand, thought she did not like this man at all. He brought out every angry and nasty part of her nature. But she trusted him. She didn't understand why, yet she did. She gave a slight nod.

Grandma Bricken turned and cut two thick slices of bread from her sourdough loaf and poured two aromatic cups of coffee from the pot simmering on the back burner. She sat the bread and cups on either side of the round kitchen table, and motioned for them to sit.

"Thank you." Ken eased his weight into the comfortable, oversized oak chair.

Kat hesitated, then sat. She faced Mr. FBI and wished she were anywhere else.

"Do you believe in good and evil, Agent Melbourne? More to the point, do you believe in God and Satan?"

Ken sighed. Before answering, he picked up the cup, blew and took a tentative sip.

"In my line of work, ma'am, I have seen a lot of evil. So, I believe in what evil man can commit, yes.

"Do I believe in the battle described in the Bible between God and Satan for men's souls—no. I think we humans must have an explanation for everything, even when there is none, enter God and the Devil. How can we describe it otherwise?"

"Well, Agent, you are wrong. Telling this tale is going to be a lot harder because of your disbelief."

Grandma Bricken closed her eyes, deep in thought or meditation, Ken couldn't tell which.

She seemed to come to a decision, and took in a deep breath. "I will tell you anyway because, whether you want to be or not, you are now a key player in the real-life legend unfolding in Ravens Cove. And you will be staying to the end, good or bad. I can feel it."

Kat knew her grandmother's intuitions well. They were never wrong. The odd new pastor called her a prophet. He said a true prophet's predictions always came true. He described Grandma Bricken to a *T*. She never, never voiced an intuition which did not come to pass. Although Kat did not often agree with Pastor Lucas, she did about her grandmother and her intuitions.

"The man you have in custody, Agent Melbourne, is not your suspect. Unfortunately, I believe it will become clear by tonight."

"He is the prime suspect. He . . ." Ken stopped in midbreath.

He came close to launching into elaborate details about the two murders, including the little-known fact they both occurred after dark. He knew confiding in her could jeopardize the investigation and his career. Her ability to rein in the Ice Queen had increased his admiration for her, which, in turn, increased his comfort-level with her. As a result, he dropped his guard and forgot his first priority— never let your emotions overtake your logic.

Grandma waived a hand in front of his far-off eyes. "Are you with me?"

Ken blinked a couple of times, smiled, and nodded.

She searched his face. Satisfied, she continued, "What you are looking for is older than the beginning of time. It is of eternity. It has visited Ravens Ravine since being thrown from heaven along with its leader, known as Lucifer, or Satan, or Beelzebub, or whatever name you wish to call it. When it is in residence, it has the power to destroy anything or anyone who comes into the ravine. To date, it has not reached its full power. It works in secret to build its strength. But I need to go backward not forward."

This story sounded all too familiar. "Has Josiah Williams been here?" Ken asked.

"Never heard of him. If he knows of this legend, it is not from me!"

"Sorry, just needed to check the facts."

"This thing, Lord I pray your protection now, Iconoclast by name, has been given power over this area to destroy. Any people who dare to live around the ravine are in jeopardy.

"The good news, if there can be good news, is Iconoclast has a limited time to complete his plan. If he succeeds, he reigns and has authority to kill all who come through here for five years.

"If the Lord allows it to prevail, and if the people of Ravens Cove do not turn to God for help, this will be a wasteland within two weeks. It will take the people first, then the animals. It will tear all living things limb from limb and snack as it wants. The screams of those souls, animals too, will make this place uninhabitable for centuries. It will be known as haunted—a cursed and desolate place."

Grandma Bricken sighed. "This beautiful town will be given over to darkness, not a sunrise again for centuries. Only blackness will cover it.

"There may be a way to block Iconoclast from ever again returning to Ravens Ravine, but none have been able to succeed. So until the end of the age of grace we now live in, until our Lord returns, or until a person or persons can be used by Jesus to defeat this horror, he has the ability to destroy and take souls for his ruler. Come Lord, Jesus."

Grandma continued, "Iconoclast needs five victims to have enough power to overtake and destroy the town and all its inhabitants. The recent deaths, and the manner in which those poor souls died, have confirmed what I already knew. Ravens Cove is in Iconoclast's territory.

"Two souls have been taken, and already the evil individuals in this town are becoming more brazen, hoping to help this malevolent force, not knowing their own destruction will come first." She shook her head.

Kat took a deep breath and exhaled. She heard the legend many times. If her grandmother had an odd, obsessive side, this was it. To her it was a truth, and no one could convince Grandma Bricken otherwise.

"So, why didn't this happen before?" Ken asked with a tone of puzzlement, not the disbelief of other outsiders.

"In 1778 a crew member of the HMS *Resolution* was found murdered in much the same way as you've seen here. His shipmates left him where they found him on what we now call Corpse Mound. By the time the Denali found him, Iconoclast had left the area. Since then, no one lived near Ravens Ravine until recent decades.

"The original settlers, my people, the Denali, respected the legend and did not settle here. The white settlers who did come, respected the Denali cultures and did not go near the ravine—it being sacred ground. Then, as is human nature, people decided there is no threat and settled here. My people included.

"The first white settlers came and stayed because they could easily sustain an existence on the abundant fish and game. Missionaries followed. They converted many of my people; my direct ancestors among them. In the past fifty years or so, people have lost their fear of the evil foe. Not so much the Denali but the whites who came to settle."

Kat blocked the tale and instead studied Ken for a reaction. She noted he was either a talented actor or his respect was genuine. Different from any other man she had known. Any suitor who she ever showed a romantic interest in ran, as if the house were going to collapse, when Grandma launched into this tale. Kat knew it was Grandma's way of producing a shotgun to make sure the prospective man in her life would treat her well. *There have been no prospects for a long time,* Kat mused.

And this man, Mr. Ego-driven from the big city and the Lower 48, is the one who passed the test. Of course, he did! The very one who repelled her as if she were a mosquito, and he was bug spray.

Kat realized she had been staring at Ken. She averted her eyes to her grandmother's face. Too late, Grandma and FBI saw it. It was her turn to blush.

Grandma Bricken leveled her gaze on Ken. There was something going on here between her beloved granddaughter and this stranger. Something they didn't even know about yet.

"Agent Melbourne, there will be more murders," she repeated, lifting her ample bulk from the chair to get the coffeepot. Kat took a full cup.

"Just half, please. I'm not much for caffeine."

Ken's job alone kept him so alert there were many sleepless nights without an added stimulant. Add a spooky story, and he might not sleep for weeks.

Grandma Bricken smiled as she poured. She liked someone who knew his own strengths and weaknesses. She looked at the clock over the sink.

"Oh, look at the time. I must get ready now. Church service this evening."

"Grandma, not again," Kat said. She felt disturbed by how much time her grandmother spent with those Bible thumpers at the new church.

"Yes, again. Tonight is a special prayer service. These murders have the town so on edge. Among other things, it is my duty to pray, with my brothers and sisters in Christ, for God to give peace and strength to each townsperson."

"How much good can a couple of old people praying do, Gram? I want you to stay home. There is a murderer out there. In fact, I will go get BC and stay here tonight."

Grandma Bricken's countenance softened. "Katrina, I am fine."

She reached down and cupped Kat's chin in her hand, lifting her face up until their eyes met. "I am so blessed to have you and your love in my life." She released Kat's chin and stroked her cheek with the back of her rough, brown hand.

Kat grabbed it and looked into her beloved grandmother's eyes. Her love, more her loyalty, yelled, *Protect her!*

Grandma took Kat in when her mom ran off with some angler from Oregon. And she didn't hesitate to make Kat her own after Kat's dad, a sailor, was killed in some far-off port by some far-off enemy.

"Please Grandma." Kat forgot Ken was in the room witnessing this tender moment.

Ken felt a tug on his heart. A need to shelter Kat overtook the desire he had felt.

Emotions are dangerous. Ken brought himself back to reality, filtering the conversation and actions of these two.

"If it makes you feel better, come and stay, Kat."

Grandma couldn't say the same for the beast Kat kept with her. It was the nastiest thing Grandma Bricken had ever seen called a pet. But it loved Kat and so Grandma accepted it, spiteful disposition and all. "And, of course, bring BC."

"I don't want you out after dark, Grandma!" Kat was insistent.

"Well, as you know, there is more dark than light this time of year. And, it is more important than anything else for me to get to church tonight."

Kat began twisting and untwisting her paper napkin, just as she did as a child when something troubled her.

"I'll tell you what, Kat, you and Agent Melbourne come with me; then you can see I'm okay until I get home."

"I don't like this idea at all! I do not want to go to church." *And I surely don't want to go with Agent Melbourne,* Kat thought.

"All or nothing, Kat. It might not be safe for just the two of us, either. I would feel better knowing we have such a strong escort." Grandma smiled. "And I do believe he must carry a gun. Right, Agent?"

"Certainly do, ma'am." He patted the belt under his coat and over his right hip.

"Do not encourage her!" Kat shot psychic darts at him, eyes flashing.

Ken caught her gaze and held it. "Your grandmother needs to be escorted. You yourself said she should not be out alone after dark. I agree. And either we both go or she's going by herself. Did I get your wishes right, Mrs. Bricken?"

"Indeed you did. Indeed you did." She winked at Ken out of view from Kat.

Kat knew she was fighting a losing battle. "Fine. I'll call Bart and tell him I won't be back this afternoon. I'm going home to pack, grab BC, and I'll be back here before you want to leave. What time is this service?"

"Six o'clock."

"Don't look so pleased with yourself, Grandma. You either, FBI! I don't like this one bit." Kat pushed back from the table, picked up her purse and headed for the door.

"We'll be here by five forty-five," Ken said. "Do not leave without us. I mean it, Mrs. Bricken. Your granddaughter is right about the danger everyone in town is facing."

"Call me Grandma, Agent Melbourne, everyone in town does."

She knew this man was the one for Kat and would be a part of her family. She felt good about it this time. All those others Kat brought to her home—few and far between as they might be—were wrong for Kat.

This one was strong and just as hardheaded, but more levelheaded and possessed a capacity for great love. The right combination for Kat, as soon as they both came to Christ. Without God's blessing, nothing would come of the relationship.

Ken never knew either of his grandmothers because he was a late-in-life baby. This woman spoke to a hole in him he didn't know existed. He cleared his throat. "Grandma." He felt ridiculous for the third time in this woman's home.

An extreme urge to catch up with Kat overcame him. He wanted to walk her somewhere, anywhere as long as he could talk to her.

"Go. She isn't but a few feet out the door by now. She's still fuming, though, so be careful of her temper, or you'll be left in the smoke of her tongue." Grandma giggled like a schoolgirl. "Go."

Ken rose and hurried for the door. He turned back. "Thank you." He flashed a conspiratorial grin at her. He didn't know why, but he knew he just made a great ally in this aged, wise, and wonderful woman.

Grandma Bricken smiled. All was going to be okay for Kat. A burden she had long carried, Kat being orphaned and alone, lifted. Alese walked to the stove and stirred the simmering meat.

A vision of Kat's mutilated body, lying on Corpse Mound, flew into her mind. Terror and despair flooded her soul.

You aren't going to be there to keep her safe. You won't keep your promise, old woman. Prevaricator's evil, malevolent laugh echoed through her mind.

"Not while I'm alive, you horrid being, not while I'm still breathing. Jesus! Take my thoughts captive now, Lord."

Prevaricator, a great deceiver, smirked. He watched his lies do their work. He felt the old biddy's faith weakening under the strain of doubt.

He relished the red and black colors snaking from her being. He opened his mouth and inhaled. Her terror tasted sweeter than any he could remember.

Alese's back straightened. "The Lord Jesus Christ rebuke you. Be gone, evil one!"

The lies flew back at him like kitchen knives.

Prevaricator somersaulted backward through the wall. He hurtled into the presence of his ruler. He quaked when it dawned on Iconoclast the mission had failed.

Enraged, Iconoclast stomped on his thin, stringy neck.

Prevaricator yowled. The yowl was decibels above the threshold of human hearing, but not above the birds. They shot into the air in search of safety.

Peace returned to Grandma Bricken. "Thank you, Lord, thank you." She checked the stove and left the kitchen to prepare for the evening service.

CHAPTER 18

BLACK CAT

K en caught up with Kat as she turned onto the street behind Grandma's house.

"May I walk you?"

"Not you, too, FBI. I can take care of myself, you know."

Kat picked up her pace, an outward expression of her need to get away from the confusion he stirred up every time she looked at him.

Ken quickened to come alongside her, which put him on a direct collision with a bike rider. The speed-demon steered his bike to avoid Kat but didn't have time to do the same for Ken.

Ken, concentrating on matching his pace to Kat's, was unaware of the impending accident.

"On your left," the bicyclist shouted.

Ken glanced up, shot sideways, tripped over a small rock and landed on his backside.

The bike rider whizzed by and became a speck on the horizon in moments.

Kat laughed so hard, tears came to her eyes. Once she could get her breath, she offered a hand.

Ken took it, but instead of pulling himself up, he pulled her down. She landed square on his stomach.

"Oomph. Sorry! Did not work out quite like I planned!" But her reaction was exactly what he hoped for. Those flashing green eyes were back.

She made a fist and punched him square on the chest as she stood.

"Ouch." He rubbed the spot to take some of the sting out of it. "You're strong, for a girl."

Kat gave a frustrated, "Huff," and took off.

By the time he could breathe again, Kat was halfway down the street. Ken caught up with her.

She made it a point to ignore him for the twenty minutes it took to walk her home. The silence made it seem like an eternity passed before he got her to her destination.

Once they arrived, Ken insisted he check the house before she went inside.

"Oh, for heaven's sake." Kat patted her pockets to find her key. She wanted to placate this guy and get some time by herself.

While he waited, Ken stood on the deck, back turned to Kat's door, taking in the awe-inspiring view. The muddy, grey inlet tossed whitecaps toward shore at an alarming rate. The breeze was gentle here, yet tinged with possible peril, evidenced by the gale force winds whipping the distant waves into a frenzy.

An active volcano, flanked by pointed, inhospitable mountains, sent puffs of steam upward. The knowledge of an imminent explosion underlined the threat of a serial killer on the loose in this off-the-map town.

Ken lived for danger and Ravens Cove contained dangers he had never known or thought about growing up in Iowa. He became an FBI agent because he loved the chase—and winning. Finding a serial killer was adrenaline-producing. He did not doubt he would win in a battle with a human being. But the possibility of earthquakes, volcanoes erupting, not to mention the moose and bear were numerous, and could trample or devour one, really spoke to Ken. This place felt more like home than anywhere he had been on earth.

As a bonus, Kat was the most electrifying woman he had ever met. His feelings were growing stronger for her and the raw beauty of this place. *I knew about earthquakes and volcanoes when I arrived. But living in Anchorage, the idea of such disasters is distant at best.* This place shouted danger.

A sharp pain brought him back to reality. Ken looked to the source of his pain. A black, short-haired cat, as green-eyed as its master, attacked his leg, claws out as if scaling a tree.

"What the ....!" Ken shook his leg in a rapid motion attempting to shake off the psychotic cat.

The homicidal feline screeched and dug in deeper seeming to enjoy the ride.

"Blast it!" *I'm going to have to shoot this thing.*

Kat tilted her head, confused at BC's more-than-normal violent reaction. "Stop moving!" She bent down and unhooked each claw.

Ken counted sixteen tugs before he was finally free.

BC's tail swished back and forth, He glared into Ken's eyes, a low growl told Ken—if BC had anything to do with it—more attacks were coming.

"Told you I was fine." She picked up BC and dropped him inside her cabin and slammed the door. "You'd better go now. BC honored you with one of his more delicate warnings."

Ken pulled Kat close, kissed her hard on the mouth, released her and headed for the steps. He looked back over his right shoulder.

Kat stood wide-eyed, staring toward the water. *He's either courageous or a fool,* she thought. No man ever risked her anger by kissing her without permission; and no man stayed on her porch or crossed her threshold, for that matter, since BC took up residence.

"You pull a stunt like that again, FBI, and I'll . . ."

"You'll what?"

"I don't know! But you'll be more than sorry."

Ken grinned and said, "Noted. I'll be here to get you at five fifteen."

Kat inhaled deeply and let out a slow, shaky breath. "If you aren't here by five-fifteen, I won't be here at five-sixteen." She turned, walked inside and slammed the door.

CHAPTER 19

PRAYERS AND PLOTS

Ken arrived at five-ten, allowing for differences in clocks. He knocked and sidestepped the second BC attack. He grabbed the cat in one arm, pulling just hard enough on the nape of his neck, like a mother cat carries its kitten, to stop the biting and clawing in its tracks. Subdued, BC lay still, except for the swishing tail.

"Enough, cat. Now off with you." Ken dropped BC ahead of him into the cabin to give himself a head start if the cat decided to come at him again.

Kat favored Ken with a look bordering on respect. "No one knows how to subdue BC but me."

She stepped out the door, closed and locked it.

"Darn." She unlocked the door, swept BC into a kennel before he could protest and grabbed the overnight bag. Balancing the bag and BC, Kat squeezed through the door and kicked it shut.

"Kat." Bart's voice came from the gravel path doubling for a driveway.

Kat and Ken turned to watch his stocky frame come up the hill to her lawn.

"Where're you off to?"

His eyes settled in challenge on Ken's face. *Possible friend or not, this guy is trouble where Kat's concerned.*

Ken returned the glare.

"We're going to get Grandma and take her to church."

Bart turned surprised eyes to Kat. "Since when do you go to church, especially the holy rollin' one?"

"Since Grandma wouldn't take no for an answer and was going to go by herself after dark. No choice."

"Stubborn. We do come by it rightly, now don't we?" he chuckled.

"We?" Ken asked.

"Well, not because this is any of your business either, FBI, but we're related. This man is not just our town's fine sheriff, he is also my first cousin."

Relief and understanding flooded Ken. He mistook family protectiveness for male competition.

"I'll walk with you."

"That's not necessary. One escort is more than enough," Kat answered.

"Probably right, KittyKat. But, we got the autopsy results and some information on the John Doe from yesterday. I want to go over them with Melbourne."

Ken lost interest in the family relationship and turned his full attention to Bart. "Listening."

"Seems our John Doe is, or was, a Mr. Theodore Dank, a homeless man, residing in and around Anchorage. Has a record for panhandling, petty theft, nothing big. Don't know what brought him this way, but I'm assuming he was looking for a warmer climate to spend the winter.

"The autopsy results were a little odd. The black stuff coming from his eyes was sulfurous in nature; the purple is some kind of plant or herb not known to Ravens Cove or even Alaska from what the ME said.

"He could have died from a variety of things, most of which seemed to occur at the same time. Among them, he had a heart attack and a both lungs were punctured by broken ribs."

"Makes sense."

"But the medical examiner could not explain the absence of skin or blood from the body. They are still looking for a reason. No immediate signs of burning or bloodletting; they are thinking acid was used to remove the skin. They'll get back to us."

They stopped at Grandma Bricken's house.

"You look beautiful!" Bart said.

Grandma Bricken beamed, then looked at the three young people standing on her porch. "My escort has increased, I see."

Kat deposited BC and her bag in the entry. With the knowledge of a frequent visitor, she grabbed a white ceramic bowl from the upper cabinet in the kitchen, filled it with water and set it on the floor.

"There, BC, you're set 'til we get back."

Grandma Bricken's warm eyes followed Kat throughout the routine. Her granddaughter's depth of love extended well beyond family to all she felt needed her. An admirable trait, although one which got Kat hurt on more than one occasion.

"Well let's be off then."

The quartet arrived at the small house-turned-church well after dark. It was a little before six.

Floor lamps and some yellow-tinted bulbs in the ceiling fixtures gave the place a warm glow. The small room smelled of fresh paint.

Grandma joined her long-time friends at the front of the building.

Kat surveyed the room and its occupants. There were new faces, too. At least ones Kat did not see when she accidentally showed up at one of her gram's many home Bible studies.

If there were twenty people, though, she'd be surprised. Still, the peace and lightness in this building made up for the sparse gathering. A feeling of security, of protection, overtook her senses.

Paul Lucas stood on the low, hand-built stage and smiled out to his flock. He took hold of the small wooden box in front of him.

"As you know, my friends, our town is under attack. Two people have lost their lives in just as many days. It is urgent we pray for our town and the safety of its residents. The Lord has told us where two or more gather in His name, He will be among them. And He has promised to answer our cries. Let us cry out to Him. He is our salvation."

A different type of meeting took place at the Congregational Alliance. A combined memorial service for Miggie Salisto and pep talk by Reverend Plotno.

Reverend Plotno considered it time to confront and disassemble the congregation of Paul Lucas. He could not do it himself, but he was sure some of his people would want to. All he needed to do was push them in the right direction. Earlier, he insisted Anita go to Lucas's church and do some snooping. She was peeved; but like a good servant, went anyway.

"I'm surprised I miss my most adoring fan," he mumbled. He wanted to see her love-struck eyes while he delivered his fiery and enlightening speech. He comforted himself knowing he would catch up with her in private, later.

"My friends, we have lost a dear brother. This, as you all know, is the second murder in two days. There is one they say who is jailed and suspected of these horrific crimes. And do you know where he was before he went to jail? Visiting Paul Lucas!"

The congregation gasped in unison.

"We have known, and I've told you for a long time, Lucas's assembly is bad for Ravens Cove! We must do something to shut it down! Any of you could be next!"

The threat of bodily harm primed them.

"I am praying, and ask you pray, for the church's destruction so no more harm will come to this town! We are in peril; I feel it!" He paused so his next statement would have its desired effect.

Atramentous was standing behind Plotno, whispering into his puppet's ear. He left his position at the door, knowing this was where he needed to be right now, no matter what Iconoclast said.

Because he left his post, he did not notice Uriel slip into a pew in the back.

"My guide has told me this!" Plotno shouted.

The rumble of belief affirmed his ploy worked.

Uriel left and flew to the man who occupied the town's lone jail cell to warn him.

Sheriff Bart left the service at Paul Lucas's church, puzzled at the hatred felt for this man by most all of the town, at least those who attended the Congregational Alliance.

"He seems harmless enough." Bart shook his head. "I'll never understand people."

Bart arrived at the office.

Josiah sat on the edge of his bed, head bent, and deep in thought.

"Here's the Bible you requested." Bart handed it through the bars.

"Thanks much." Josiah gave an appreciative smile.

Bart made sure Josiah had water and blankets for the long night ahead, and headed out the door and onto the street. A large black lump caught his attention.

Who the heck left their trash in the street? Some in this town can't seem to get with the program. I'll have to issue another warning in the morning. He walked toward the trash to pick it up and throw it in one of the cans behind the building.

But it wasn't trash. It was a flock of ravens, dead in a heap, right outside the Trash Bin, the adult store. He leaned over and touched one. Still warm.

"Who would do such a thing?"

Maybe the murderer? he answered himself.

But if my prime suspect is in jail, my theory doesn't hold water.

"Not the murderer," Bart said aloud.

Bart headed back to the office for trash bags, cleaned up the carcasses and, an hour after he planned to, started for home.

The Northan twins were taking a walk on the path leading to Ravens Ravine.

"Those ravens won't be making any noise or stealing our food anymore," Jonathan said.

"There'll be more of them."

"Then, we'll do it again. It's a community service—right?"

"I guess so."

Joseph looked down, saw a pretty arrowhead, and snatched it up, hoping Jonathan didn't notice.

"Let me see!"

Joseph opened his hand; the pretty thing was pulsing in colors. "I want it!"

"No."

They got into one of their regular fights and, before they knew it, tumbled into Ravens Ravine. A victorious growl resounded throughout the surrounding countryside. Every canine, every wolf howled. Blood red-smoke streamed upward out of the ravine.

Josiah's head shot up from his Bible. "The fourth victim has been taken!" *How? There should be just one a night.*

"Only one left then, only one day, before Iconoclast is released to destroy Ravens Cove and its people."

"God help them, and God help me!" He prayed.

Kat, Ken, and Grandma Bricken stopped when they heard the rising chorus of canine voices.

Grandma's spirit became troubled. "I'm not sure what has happened, but it is something awful. The howls are a sign of unrest and precede imminent destruction."

As soon as Grandma Bricken opened the door, BC launched himself off the entry hall table. He landed in Ken's arms.

Grandma turned the lights on.

"What a sight!" She couldn't help but smile, even knowing a supreme evil was present in her town and wanting to destroy it.

There sat BC. Curled up and holding tight to Ken's right arm, looking like a hairy football with claws. And he showed no signs of letting go.

"What the he—" Ken remembered Grandma's earlier warning about foul language.

BC's green eyes were as large as saucers, trumped only by the size of his tail, which was returning to its normal size as he relaxed. He cuddled deeper into Ken's arm. Without giving it a thought, Ken encircled BC with the other arm, comforting the very being who tried to maim him for life a few hours earlier.

"Give him to me," Kat said and reached for BC.

Black Cat left the safety of Ken's arms for hers. His nose and eyes disappeared into the crook of her arm.

"I've never seen BC afraid of anything," Grandma said.

"Did you notice," concerned she was seeing things, Kat hesitated.

"Notice what?" Ken asked.

"The weird, red fog coming from the ravine?"

Her question got both Ken's and Grandma's attention.

"Yes," they said in unison.

Relieved, she had not been imagining things, "Well, I'm still not saying the ravine legend is real, but the howling, the red fog, and a fearful BC, has me wondering. I feel a need to talk to Mr. Josiah Williams."

"I've had a hard time convincing myself he acted alone," Ken responded. "If he didn't commit the murders, he sure knows a lot about them. And, how would he—unless he knew who committed them?"

"The jail is locked up for tonight. But I happen to have a key." Kat reached into her purse and produced it.

Ken made a grab for it and missed.

"Not without me, FBI." Not waiting for permission, Kat slid an unhappy BC into her grandma's arms.

"You'll be safe with BC."

"We'll be fine. You do what you need to and do it fast! We have twenty-four hours to find a way to stop this thing."

CHAPTER 20

HERALDS OF DESTRUCTION

Iconoclast stood with his back against the oozing, pea-green wall on the north side of the ravine. His most trusted fighters surrounded him in a semicircle, the growing number of demons encircled them, spanning the ravine to the slimed walls on the south side.

Iconoclast grinned. "Just like all good vultures, you smelled blood and came from around this puny world to feast on those who took it upon themselves to live here. This is very good!"

He looked at his captains—Gambogian, Caitiff, Venenose, Bruit, Trepaner, and Prevaricator.

Atramentous and Profligacy were absent by his orders, guarding Plotno and his assembly—a higher priority.

These eight were with him in defeat in Josiah Williams' horrid small town and in near-victory over the village in China.

"One man of God stood between us and complete conquest at the battle in China. Not this time! Tomorrow we will feast," he rumbled, the strength of souls taken carrying the growl high and far.

The twins increased his power threefold. They were considered as one, coming from the same egg, so he could take two at one time and be ahead of schedule. It did not break the rules, set so long ago, by Satan. Satan loved to test those under his command and demanded they follow the rules. *And how I enjoy out tricking the Great Trickster.*

"To ensure the desolation and so these humans will be given into our hands, I am required to have one join us, by this mortal's own free will. One who I must wrestle from the Holy One's hands. Without this fifth victim, we lose."

The twins, now what some would term ghosts, along with John Doe (aka Theodore Dank) and Miggie, were among those who joined Iconoclast.

"Ah, the obedient slaves all mortals were intended to be." Iconoclast said. "You dead souls will be useful in stirring up the terror and confusion needed to divide and overcome the inhabitants of Ravens Cove. Go out, visit many. You are the heralds of the destruction to come. If you find the one I speak of, bring the human to me."

The ghouls did as commanded. They no longer possessed free will. Their days of choice ended when they allowed their souls to be tempted and tricked into service to Iconoclast.

Their main desire now, if you could call it a desire, was to have as many souls as possible join them in misery. They screamed and screeched, repeating the sounds made the instant they met their fates. The moment of death never left their tortured minds. The bloodied, oozing-eyed minions of Iconoclast flew upward in a purple haze, taking the deepening red mist with them, off to the town to wreak terror.

Atramentous settled over the door of the Congregational Alliance. Hearing the screech of the ghouls, his head-shaped fog snapped around until his chin rested on what would be a spine.

"Iconoclast took his fourth victim. Soon I will not cover this door. I will be released. Then I will take the entire church and its loyal patrons." In anticipation of the feast to come, red saliva dripped off the one concrete thing in this monster, his knife-teeth.

The dark chasm of a mouth opened and screeched, "Go, my beauties, fly to your destinations. Wreak havoc; set fear in the hearts of these mortals, so much fear they are stricken and paralyzed. So much easier to take; so much easier to enjoy at leisure, with horror as the tenderizer."

CHAPTER 21

UNWELCOME VISITORS

Cassandra Martin stayed late at her beauty shop. "The Right Reverend Plotno must be serviced when he wants or my shop would be boycotted—jerk! Thank goodness you were finally satisfied, Reverend," she whispered to herself, watching him stride up the street.

As she closed the door, she felt, rather than heard, a presence behind her.

She stiffened, hand still holding the key in the shop's lock. "Turn, Cassie, turn."

She knew this voice. "Miggie? The sheriff said you were dead." She whirled around to see her friend, thought dead and now alive!

Cassie spun into a sight her mind could not accept. The face was blood red; the eyes were black, seeping purple. She caught her breath but too late. The stench caught in her throat, and she began to throw up and couldn't stop.

Miggie howled in laughter.

Cassandra dropped to her knees in front of him—still dry-heaving uncontrollably.

Miggie laughed louder when she started to sob.

My job is done here. He shot up, black and blood trailing behind him.

Kat and Ken turned onto Main Street. They walked side by side because he would not let her get ahead of him.

Give me some room—please! she thought.

They saw the body in front of the salon at the same time.

Ken took off in a full run.

Kat froze in place for a moment, shook herself and ran after him.

Ken dropped to his knees and checked Cassandra's neck for a pulse.

Kat, breathing hard, caught up. She inhaled. The stench caught in her throat. She turned and dry-heaved.

Ken reached into his pocket and brought out a small, round travel jar. "Put some of this under your nose."

For the first time Kat could remember, she did as she was told, then looked at the jar. "Cold salve?" she said. "Huh. I've never felt as grateful for this petroleum-based mentholated ointment as I do now."

The smell was still somewhat there; but the menthol overpowered it. She handed the jar back to Ken. "Thanks."

He took the jar and smiled up at her.

Kat caught her breath. She could bask in its warmth for the rest of her life.

"She's alive," Ken said. "Sure threw up a lot, though." He waived the Mentholatum under the woman's nose to try and bring her back. "No smelling salts. This will do in a pinch." He shook Cassandra.

Her eyes opened, and she screamed.

Ken took hold of both her shoulders and squeezed. "You're safe, you're safe," he cooed as to a small child.

Cassandra's glazed eyes focused on the handsome, dark-haired stranger. She screamed louder. "You're going to kill me. You're going to kill me!" She struggled.

Ken held Cassie steady to keep her from rolling in her own vomit.

"Cassie, stop!" Kat yelled.

Cassandra tilted her head backward, recognized Kat, and relaxed.

"What happened?" Kat asked.

"Miggie." Cassandra trembled and began to sob.

"Yes, Miggie's dead, Cassie."

"No. He was here. He called my name. He looked so ..." she began to heave again at the memory.

Ken, still holding Cassie's shoulders, watched as Kat fell to one knee and began smoothing Cassandra's hair.

"Shhh. Take a deep breath, and tell me what happened."

"It was Miggie, Kat, he came to see me. He looked horrible but the voice was Miggie's. You know I know his voice, Kat."

Kat nodded her head.

"They were an item." She whispered to Ken over Cassie's head.

Cassandra turned into Kat's coat and wept.

"Ouch," Ken mouthed back.

"You believe me, don't you, Kat? Please tell me you believe me!" Cassie's voice rose, afraid she was going crazy. Afraid *Kat* would think she was going crazy.

"I believe you believe it. I know how much you cared for him." Kat had no idea why Cassie chose to love Miggie, but then there were many mysteries in the world.

Cassandra looked up at Kat, mascara streaming down her cheeks, mixing with her rose blush and ivory foundation. The combination looked like a bad watercolor.

"It's the truth. God's truth." Cassandra's voice trailed off. She stared into the darkness.

"We need to get her to a hospital," Ken said.

Both Kat and Cassie whipped their heads to Ken, surprised.

"No! I'm fine. I just want to get home, take a hot bath and forget this ever happened ... if forgetting is even possible."

"I urge you to get a good once over by a doctor," Ken answered.

"She says she's fine," Kat said. "I believe her. Here, take her keys, go into her shop and get her a glass of water. If she keeps it down, we'll call her roommate, Caroline, to come over and get her. If not, we'll call Doctor Billings and have him come look her over. Agreed?"

Knowing he was outnumbered and would just waste valuable time by arguing, he took the keys.

When Cassandra kept the water down and sat up without assistance, Ken admitted she was okay.

He handed Kat his phone. She looked at him as if he were from another planet when he held out the cell.

"Look around you. How hard is it to get ahold of someone?" Kat spread her arms wide and turned, first toward North Main, then South Main, to emphasize her point. "I mean, how hard is it?"

Ken pointed to the phone.

Kat dialed.

Caroline arrived ten minutes later. "I'd have been here sooner, but it took five minutes to find my sweats." Caroline guided Cassie to the car and whisked her away.

"I don't know what is going on here, but one thing I know for sure is Cassie would never let anyone see her unless she is coiffed and dressed to the nines."

"A hallucination," Ken said, not as convincing as he would have liked. In the last twenty-four hours, he saw enough of the unexplainable to last him a lifetime. Still, hallucination was the most logical answer. Or some horrible joke played on Cassie.

Josiah passed the time by looking out the small jail window, pondering the smoky darkness gathering to the south.

"Old man." A voice, no, two blended voices, came from within his cell.

Josiah's spirit knew what he would see before he looked. "In your name, Jesus, hide me in your righteousness. Let this evil have no power over me. You have allowed them to come here. Show me why."

Josiah turned, the straightness of his body, the heat in his eyes belying his age and the heaviness he carried with him always.

"What are your names? In the name of Jesus, I command you, answer."

The twins thought Iconoclast to be their lone master. They were shocked when they had no choice but to answer this horrid little mortal.

"In life, we were called Joseph and Jonathan."

"Your last name in life, what was it?" Josiah demanded.

The twins hesitated but could not stop from answering. They felt their power draining as they answered him. "Northan," they said in unison, their voices merging to make a putrid, dripping noise.

The sound reminded Josiah of blood being let from a carcass to prepare the meat for packaging.

"How did you meet the demise of your physical bodies? Joseph answer!" he demanded.

The twins power lessened when not working and speaking together. Joseph felt the drain again. He felt pain. The light surrounding this puny man was blinding his already dead eyes.

"Iconoclast tricked us!"

"Your own greed tricked you!"

Jonathan stayed silent, unable to talk until commanded to do so. Terror flooded his being; an emotion he never felt in life. Now, the anguish he once inflicted on God's innocent creatures was tearing at his non-existent flesh. He could feel each one he killed, the most recent of which was the strongest. He experienced the suffering of the ravens as their internal organs melted, and they bled to death. The pain was unbearable. He needed to run but could not.

Jesus, protect me. "Who is this Iconoclast?"

"Our commander. The one whose mission it is to destroy this insignificant horrible little town and its inhabitants. That's who!" Joseph regained strength when he remembered why he came here.

"Enough of you now, Joseph Northan! Speak, Jonathan! Tell me the names of Iconoclast and his underlings. Name all you know!"

Jonathan and Joseph were ordered not to divulge any names. He would be punished if Iconoclast discovered he told this human. Jonathan worked to hold his tongue, to divest his thoughts of the names but could not.

He blurted out, "Atramentous, Gambogian, Caitiff, Venenose, Bruit, Trepaner, Prevaricator and Profligacy. These are all I know. I swear!"

"Swear not in front of me. Be gone. Go back to your leader, and tell him I am here. He knows me. I await the battle."

The twins flew up through the jail cell and dropped like meteors into the ravine.

Kat unlocked the door to the sheriff's office, the bell's tinny ring much louder in the silent, deserted place.

Ken stepped through behind her. He caught his breath, then he covered his nose. "Do you smell something?"

Kat tapped the side of her nose, reminding Ken of the menthol treatment minutes earlier. "Not really."

"Lucky you. This place smells like rotting meat. Did someone forget to put out the garbage? It'll draw rats, you know."

"The garbage was emptied earlier. And the most recent sighting of a rat in Ravens Cove was yesterday." She turned innocent eyes upward to Ken. "Even BC could only take a chunk out of it, it was so big."

Ken glared down into those cat-green eyes. He forced himself to turn away, before he just grabbed this woman and kissed her again.

"Katrina Agnes Tovslosky."

They heard her name being called from the back, from the direction of the jail cell.

"Stop calling my full name! How do you know it anyway?" Kat's voice trailed behind her as she headed for the cell. "Almost no one knows my middle name, especially some stranger to Ravens Cove!"

"Agnes?"

Kat scowled at Ken. "If you *ever* say my middle name again, you'll wish BC had finished the job!" She marched forward.

"I'll take my chances," Ken answered.

Kat stopped in front of the bars, arms akimbo, turning an *I can melt you by pure will alone,* look on Josiah.

Josiah returned an open and fearless gaze.

Even through the Mentholatum, Kat now smelled the stench. It was emanating from the cell. She scrunched her nose, then relaxed it to try and hide the disgust.

Josiah smiled. "The smell is not me, Katrina. "I had a visitor ... two visitors this evening."

"They need to see Doc Billings," was all Kat could think of to answer.

"Wouldn't help, ma'am. They are far beyond any help mortals can offer."

Ken walked up and stopped just behind Kat's left shoulder, so close she could feel the warmth of his body.

"Who are beyond help, Mr. Williams?"

"Well the names they gave me, at least their names in life, are Joseph and Jonathan Northan. Twins I believe."

"Jonathan and Joseph? How did they get in here? They are not our most model citizens. In fact, they are a violent couple of siblings. Are you hurt?"

"They could not hurt me, but thank you for asking." Josiah's smile disappeared. "They are dead."

"Almost the stupidest thing I've ever heard." Kat turned to Ken. "I saw them walking by my grandma's home, heads together, conspiring something horrible I'm sure, as we were going to get her for church."

"They are dead, I assure you. They were sent to threaten me, no doubt, by their leader, named Iconoclast."

"What did you say?" Ken and Kat spoke at the same time.

"Iconoclast. Do you know the name?"

Kat felt the hair rising on the back of her neck. Her grandmother just shared this name with Ken a few hours ago. Many knew the legend, but Grandma held the name close, as did her mother and grandmother before her. The unease in Kat's stomach grew.

"Iconoclast. The demon sent to destroy this town and everyone who resides in it. Anyway, you will find their bodies at the top of Ravens Ravine, just as you did the others. Go see for yourself. But make sure the sheriff is with you, along with another member of the town, I would suggest Pastor Lucas. The evil is growing—it's gained immense strength, and it is emanating from the ravine."

"I can't take a pastor to a crime scene!"

"Suit yourself, but you'd be far better off with him than without him. Come back to see me when you're finished. I'll be here." Josiah laughed at his own joke.

"I will," Ken answered. He wrenched his cell phone from his pocket and hit speed dial where he'd entered Bart's number earlier in the day.

"Williams says there are more bodies. Something about being visited by ghost twins."

"Where are you? And how did you talk to Williams?"

Kat heard "Williams" and "How" and covered the phone.

"He's going to be really ticked I let you in the office without his knowledge," she whispered to Ken.

"What do you want to do?" Ken mouthed back.

Kat took the phone. "Hey, Bart. Funny thing about this Williams, Bart, he knew the name of the thing only Grandma knows."

"Ok? Still didn't answer my question."

Kat hurried on, "And he told us the Northan twins are dead. Said they visited him tonight."

She rolled her eyes at Ken and circled her ear with her index finger several times, "Crazy," she mouthed to Ken. "I told him I saw them this afternoon, but he insisted they are dead, lying at the top of the ravine just like the other two victims."

"This had better not be one of your infamous jokes, Kat!"

"I would never joke about a suspected murder or anything else so horrible!"

"Right, well, I'm warning you just in case. I'll meet you at the office."

If this is true, Bart thought, *the man must have an accomplice. It would have been easy enough to get the info to Williams via the glass and barred window above the cell. A written note would have done the trick. But how would he have known the twins' names? No one in Ravens Cove carried much ID. Why bother? No one drove much; everyone knew everyone and everyone pretty much paid cash, except the tourists.*

"I don't know how, but I'm going to find out!" Bart said. He caught hold of his gun belt, cinching it in place. He grabbed his weapon, holstered it and headed for the door.

What met Bart stopped him in his tracks. Bart's ruddy complexion drained to pale white.

"Sheriff." A toothless chasm of a mouth gurgled his name. Richard Pantino bowed.

"I see you remember me. Good. Just want to say thanks for nothin.' I made this town home. It was your job to protect my family! Where were you when my wife and small children were tortured, then murdered? Where?"

The guilt and shame of failing to rescue Dana Pantino and her children, the subsequent suicide of Richard Pantino, and his inability to protect the current residents of Ravens Cove poured in on Bart. Guilt and despair boiled to the surface.

"You're a loser, always been a loser, always will be a loser, Bartholomew Andersen. And, Loser..." the ghost held up dripping, decaying fingers in an L, "your town is ours and you can't do anything to stop it! Back off, *loser*, or you'll wish you were dead before you ever meet your new boss!" Pantino struck like a rattlesnake and bit Bart's arm with his demon teeth.

A black mist materialized beside Pantino. It twisted into a thin rope and dove into Bart's arm.

Bart's mouth opened wide in a silent, terrified scream. He couldn't move or speak.

The ghoul launched through the roof, going for his next victim.

Bart found the presence of mind to slam the door. He slid down behind it, legs unable to hold him.

The horror of finding the Pantino children flooded Bart—the small, mutilated corpses. The oozing wounds on Dana Pantino's corpse... her severed head.

He hid his eyes behind the palms of his hand and sobbed. "I am a loser, the biggest of them all."

Bart began fingering his gun. He snapped it free from the holster, playing with the hilt. It was comforting. He pulled the gun from the holster, and stared down the barrel.

CHAPTER 22

THE ATTACK

"You must go now, Katrina and Kenneth. Go now!"

Kat and Ken heard Josiah, as plain as if he were in the room with them, not closed in behind the door leading to his tiny cell. They both jumped up and ran back to the cell.

Josiah was holding onto the bars with white knuckles.

"Go where?"

"To the sheriff's home. He's in danger! Go now!"

Neither of them questioned Josiah. They knew Bart was late. They rushed from the jail, Kat leading the way up the street to a house kitty-corner from Pastor Lucas' residence.

The lights were on. The door was shut. Kat jogged up the old wooden steps on the narrow, wood-planked covered deck, long ago painted grey. She slipped on something and started falling. Before she could even think to be scared, her head was going for a hard, concussion-producing, hit. She felt her arm yank upward right before her skull met the wood.

"Ouch!" She was sure her arm was dislocated.

Ken grabbed her and pulled her forward against him, somehow managing to get in front of her and the slick, purple-black, sulfur-smelling liquid oozing from the welcome mat at the door. He held her closer. Kat let him.

She smelled like vanilla and musk. The combination was heady. For a moment, Ken forgot where they were. In this moment, only she existed.

He fought for focus. He pulled back and looked down at the ooze standing atop the mat, and his mood changed. "This looks like the stuff I saw coming from Miggie Salisto's eyes."

He grabbed latex gloves from his jacket pocket along with a cotton-tipped swab and a jar.

Kat couldn't believe what she saw. *Talk about prepared.*

"What else you got in your jacket, an autopsy kit? Bet you were a boy scout, huh?"

Ken crouched over the pungent gel. He looked up. "Eagle Scout."

"Well that answers that." Kat watched as he went to work on the goo she wouldn't have gone near with a ten-foot pole, as her grandmother was fond of saying.

She knocked on Bart's door, then tried the handle. The door was unlocked, but it wouldn't budge.

"Bart? BART!" Kat's voice rose in alarm.

Ken stood and tried the door. "The door's jammed. Is there another way in?"

"Back door." Kat started running.

Ken overtook her. If Bart was injured—or worse—dead, he wanted to get there before Kat did.

He made it to the door, opened it and entered. What he saw sent a cold chill up his spine.

Bart stared down the barrel of a .357 Magnum—seemingly transfixed by it.

Ken heard him muttering eerily, "*Loser.* Always was, always am, always will be, *loser*," over and over again. The hair on Ken's arms rose to attention.

"Bart," Ken whispered, taking a step forward.

Kat slid in behind Ken, stopped just short of knocking him forward and then looked to the right of Ken's bulk. Her cousin, her beloved macho cousin, sat in a heap on the floor, staring at a gun.

Kat gasped, a sob escaping her. She retreated behind Ken, leaned on him and tried to gather her thoughts.

"What do we do?" she whispered to Ken's back.

Ken reached behind and gently touched her right arm. "Just breath. We'll get through this, Kat."

Kat relaxed in response to his touch and words. A loud knock on the door jarred her back to defense mode.

The noise didn't faze Bart.

If he had jumped, Ken thought, *it would be the end.*

"Go find out who's at the door, Kat."

She wanted to protest but thought better of it. She slipped out the back, around the side of the house and looked over the deck banister.

"Pastor Lucas?"

Paul turned to her voice.

"What are you doing here? If you need the sheriff, I'll get him to you as soon as I can. He's not feeling well at the moment."

"I believe the sheriff needs me, Ms. Tovslosky."

"I don't understand what you mean, Pastor."

"I know you don't agree with my beliefs. But right now, all I can tell you is I was on my way to bed when I felt an overwhelming urge to come here. Bart is in imminent danger, isn't he?"

"As I said, he isn't feeling very well."

"Miss Tovslosky, you know it's more, and so do I. Bart is under spiritual oppression, if not a possession. He is going to kill himself if we don't help him."

Kat stared at Paul. "What is going on in this town? People know things they shouldn't. It's like the whole place is bugged and the information is getting to you and Josiah Williams. Two of the most— sorry Pastor— unbelievable, if not just plain fanatical, people in Ravens Cove."

"No offense taken, Kat. In answer to your question: God. God is working here."

Kat searched Paul's face. Seeing only earnestness in his eyes, she motioned Paul to the back of the house. "Come with me."

"Has the sticky-stuff on the porch been there long?" he asked.

"No."

Paul nodded. "I've seen this liquid and its source in a vision. We are up against great evil."

He removed his Bible from his coat and began praying. "The battle has begun, Jesus. I trust in the armor of God to surround us. Amen."

Kat shook her head and led Paul into the house through the back door.

Ken stood right where Kat left him.

"He's not aware of us," he said as Kat tiptoed up beside him.

Tears filled Kat's eyes to see her tough, strong, protector in this unrecognizable lump on the floor.

Pastor Lucas walked up beside Kat. "Peace to this house," he said in a firm voice.

Bart stopped muttering, but continued to examine the barrel of his .357 Magnum.

The three of them created a human wall filling the large open doorway leading from Bart's kitchen to his living room.

Ken shot a questioning look at the new arrival. He knew he should be surprised, but there had been so many strange events in the last two days, he didn't give Lucas's appearance more than a second thought.

Pastor Lucas opened a well-worn, leather-bound Bible and began to read.

Ken gave a resigned shrug. "Can't hurt," he whispered.

Paul closed the Bible with a snap. He straightened, resolute in a decision and walked forward.

Ken wanted to tackle the pastor, safety being his main concern. But he knew the situation could go from bad to worse if he did. He stood helpless and watched Paul stride over to Bart.

"Bartholomew Andersen, look at me."

Bart sat motionless.

"In the name of Jesus, Bartholomew, look at me."

Bart raised hollow, unseeing eyes in the direction of the voice.

Paul noticed a red stain on Bart's flannel shirtsleeve. The stain was enlarging at an alarming rate.

"Do you want help, Bartholomew? Do you want me to help you?" Bart's eyes focused for a moment. He nodded before the glaze returned. Paul motioned Ken and Kat forward.

They didn't move.

"Come here, we must do this in agreement. If any of us is unwilling to call upon God to help Bart, we will fail."

Ken watched Bart's grip loosen on the gun. He took a chance and lunged forward, pushing Bart's hands up with one arm and grabbing for the gun with the other.

Bart retightened his grip.

Paul cried out, "Jesus, in your name, help Ken."

Ken felt a surge of strength. He pulled upward again.

Bart's grip loosened but not before his finger found the trigger.

Ken pushed the gun toward the wall as it fired, just missing Ken's face and grazing Bart's.

The gun bounced once before it skidded to a halt half beneath Bart's old brown couch.

"Too close for comfort," Ken said, voice shaking, adrenaline and strength beyond Ken's understanding still coursing through him.

Kat ran over and grabbed the gun. She tucked it behind her back. Kat returned to Ken's side, truly relaxing for the first time since arriving. She looked at Bart's arm, the blood turning a nasty brown, the arm swelling.

"We have to get him to the hospital."

Paul shook his head. "A hospital won't help unless we first deal with his soul. We must pray to bring him back. He might resist, but we must lay hands on him. Are you two willing to do it?"

Kat answered, "Not to be disrespectful, but to be honest, Pastor, I'm uneasy with this holy roller stuff. Gram tried to get me into it at a young age. I gave it a shot but didn't really feel anything.

"I ended up believing the dancing in the aisles, laying on of hands, and speaking in tongues to be a result of group hysteria. Group conscience can be powerful. And now you are asking me to do something I think is fake."

"I'm asking you to take a leap of faith," Paul said.

"I'm not sure what's going on in this crazy town with its weird happenings," Ken said, "but I'm willing to give it a shot." He put his hand on Bart.

Bart didn't move.

Kat looked at Bart and whispered, "I'd do anything for you, you big lout." She laid her right hand on Bart's head.

Paul followed suit, putting one hand on Bart's head and the other over the oozing wound.

"In the name of Jesus, Bartholomew Andersen, who attacked you?"

"Corpse Lights," he whispered. His eyes flew open in remembrance of something horrible.

Paul looked at Kat and Ken for an explanation.

Ken shrugged.

The light of recognition dawned in Kat's eyes. *Another legend. For Pete's sake, do they ever end? Look what superstition did to you, Cous. Then again, the psychology of the human mind is complex. I'll play along.*

"Corpse Light is an ethereal ball of light—ghost as some might say. In the story, it is described as a lost or wandering soul, denied entry into both heaven and hell. It wanders the night and tries to lure people to their destruction. I have no idea why he made it plural; and I have no idea why it came out of his mouth."

Kat's eyes fell on her beloved cousin. She fought back the tears threatening to fall since seeing Bart moments before.

Who did you see, Bart? Who did this to you? Was it those stupid twins? They'll wish they hadn't been born! she thought.

As if reading her mind and feelings, Paul put a hand over hers.

Kat calmed and focused.

Paul moved close to Bart. "Bart, you have been attacked; you were attacked by a force which is not physical."

Bart nodded in agreement.

"Bart, you are not crazy. Jesus is here to work through us to bring you back."

The name of Jesus brought a sudden flicker to Bart's empty eyes.

Paul took his hand off Kat's and placed it back on Bart's head. He closed his eyes and bent his head.

Kat and Ken did the same.

"Spirit what is your name? In the name of Jesus, I command you answer."

Bart lifted his head in defiance but stayed silent.

Paul stared into Bart's empty, black irises. "Again, I command you in the name of Jesus to answer!"

An eerie, malicious grin covered Bart's face. He tried to struggle but couldn't move.

The wound spurted tar-colored fluid.

Bart's mouth opened but a foreign, high screech of a voice came from his lips. "What does a name matter?"

"Your name!"

"Trepaner," it sneered. "Stupid man, I am Trepaner!" The words gurgled through Bart's clenched teeth. He spat at Paul.

"Be still—Now!" Paul commanded.

A deep growl answered Paul.

"Enough! The Lord Jesus Christ rebuke you, Trepaner. Come out of this man, in Jesus' name!"

An ebony mist, smelling of rotted flesh and excrement, rose from Bart's chest.

Kat inched backward.

"Stand your ground!" Paul told her.

Kat willed herself to move forward again.

"What kind of sickness does he have?" Ken whispered.

"It is no sickness of man. That is a demon," Paul answered, then focused on Trepaner.

"Be gone! Go back to your master and tell him the battle is lost. Jesus will not allow him to take this man or this town."

"We'll see, stupid mortal, we'll see. This is my master's domain. It is not yours!"

"This earth was given to man, not to you and your master! God has written it, and so it is true! *Be gone!*"

Trepaner screeched and rocketed upward, out through the roof and back to the ravine.

Unable to rebel against the command of this man of God, he said to Iconoclast, "The man of God says you will lose."

Iconoclast's roar could be heard from the center of the earth to the heavens. He gathered Trepaner in his paw, rolled the black mist into a ball and threw him through the earth's crust into the spirit world of hell.

"How dare this stupid messenger of the Holy One threaten me! I will destroy him, and all he loves, first!"

Iconoclast turned his back to his captains to hide the worry etched in his brow. Though he wouldn't admit it to his underlings, Iconoclast realized he was up against more than he'd thought. For a moment he felt a little of the fear he caused so many over the centuries.

Bart's eyes focused on Kat, then Ken and Paul.

"What are you doing here?" he growled.

He looked around and saw where he was. "What am I doing on the floor?"

Kat smiled, relief pouring over her like a wave.

"Wipe the grin off your face, KittyKat," Bart said.

"You're a big bonehead, Bartholomew Nelson Andersen!" She grinned wider.

Bart's expression said it all. "I'll let you get away with using my middle name—this once. I feel kind of puny."

"We need to get you to the hospital," Kat answered.

"Why? I don't feel that bad."

"Your arm is injured, Bart. Do you remember how it happened?" she asked.

Bart glanced at his arm and saw the stain on the flannel sleeve. Puzzled, Bart said, "For the life of me, I don't know how I got this grease on my shirt."

"Your arm, Bart. Look at your arm!"

Bart rolled up the sleeve. "This does not look like a hospital issue. Don't you think you're overreacting?"

Kat followed Bart's eyes. She cocked her head to the left and squinted, afraid of what horrible injury lay beneath the fabric. Her eyes popped open. She saw red streaks, outlining a dark purple oval. As Kat watched, the purple and red started to be disappear.

"What the ...? Your wound was much more serious. I know it was."

"You need sleep KittyKat, or maybe glasses," Bart said.

"I'm not the one on the floor in a heap!" she quipped.

"Can you tell us what happened?" asked Ken.

Bart thought, his mood darkened. A look of fear flickered across his features. "Suffice it to say those Northan twins are going to see a jail cell, and soon."

Bart stood, a bit unsteady but regaining his strength with each breath.

"Well, we need to see if you can arrest those twins or if they are beyond your help at this point," Ken said.

"They have to be around; at least one of them was here! Looking ghastly but here! After I arrest them, I'll have a word with our prime suspect. He can tell us who his accomplice is. I want this finished once and for all." Bart stormed out.

Kat watched him disappear into the night. "He shouldn't be alone." She dashed after him.

Ken said, "I'm not leaving her alone, coming Lucas?"

"Lead the way."

They caught up with Kat and headed for the Northan place.

CHAPTER 23

A SECRET WEAPON

The twins' house was vacant. Lights were on and the door unlocked, as was the custom of Ravens Cove.

"Not here, but I'll find them. You bet I'll find them." Bart stomped down the street in search of his quarry.

"Why don't we go to the top of the ravine, just to humor me?" Ken asked.

Bart stopped. "Fine." He made a quick left turn, power-walking up Main Street to the path skirting the ravine and the river, ending at the inlet.

He turned. "Kat, I don't want you to come with us. Just in case. And, Pastor Lucas, I don't want you to come, either."

Paul stood his ground. "With all due respect, Sheriff, I know you don't believe you were possessed. But you were. And from what I understand is happening here, you need more than guns to fight this adversary. You need God, and you need prayer. My specialty. So, think of me as your secret weapon."

"He helped us a lot with you, Bart, you can't deny it," Ken said.

"I don't want to let anyone else get hurt—murdered for that matter!

So, if you want the Pastor to come along, and if anything happens to him, it's on you!" Bart turned. "Kat, I'm walking you to Grandma's house. Now!"

"We go together," Ken answered.

Kat took a step forward, then stopped. "Don't get me wrong, guys, I'm grateful for the escort. But I'm finding it hard to make much progress because the two of you—she pointed to Bart, then Ken— are holding my arms and Pastor Paul is walking on my heels."

"Stop complaining," Bart answered.

Kat sighed and started off again feeling like a toddler with mom and dad protecting her against a fall. She motioned to Grandma Bricken's house with her right hand. "We're here. Let me go."

Ken, Bart and Paul watched her walk inside and waited until they heard the door lock click. They headed to the ravine.

Kat leaned on the door, both palms extended against it. *I've never felt so suffocated by good intentions in my life.*

When she heard their footsteps and voices fading, Kat pushed herself off the door, went into the kitchen, sat at the comforting table and began to pour out the evening's events to Grandma Bricken.

All three men, almost up the hill to the hag tree, heard Trepaner's scream—a death scream.

"Moose lost to a wolf, I'm sure," Bart said, not instilling any confidence in himself or the others.

They continued up the rise.

It was a moonless night. The cloud cover ensured it.

Bart took the lead. He yelled when his foot hit a large substance and tripped.

Paul caught him before he went face down into the ravine.

"Thank you!"

Paul reached into his pocket. The jingle of keys preceded the flash of a small penlight which illuminated a foot.

Everything went dark again when the key ring plopped to the ground.

A bigger light replaced it. Bart scanned the flashlight up and down the obstacle he stumbled over.

"I guess I won't be arresting the Northan twins after all."

The two lay face-to-face, grinning into each other's purple and black eye sockets. In this light, they looked to be one body with two faces.

Paul pointed to their eyes. "It's the same junk I saw on your front porch."

Bart ignored him, went for his gun, and came up empty-handed. Ken took the cue and pulled his.

Bart shone the light all around the ravine, the dark swallowing anything beyond a few feet away.

They listened. No footsteps. In fact, nothing was moving, not even the trees.

"The guy couldn't have gotten far," Ken said.

"Nope."

"It's not a guy," Paul commented.

"You think it was a woman?" Bart asked.

"I mean whatever did this wasn't human."

"Okay. That's it. Pastor Paul, I believe you have done all you can here. Why don't you go home?"

A low, bone-chilling growl rose from the ravine. "Yes, leave, Man of God! You can do nothing here."

Ken and Bart shivered from the sudden drop in temperature.

"On second thought, maybe you'd better stay," Bart said.

"You remember what happened, don't you, Sheriff?"

Bart nodded, the memories rushing back like a bad dream relived. "I had a nervous break."

"No. You were possessed."

"Yeah, right."

"Who came to see you tonight?"

"Richard Pantino, a suicide victim."

Ken snapped his head around to Bart. He opened his mouth to encourage Bart to go home and rest. He shut it again.

Bart watched Ken's response. "Told you. Nervous break."

"My first thought. But, since I can't explain why you were a babbling lump on the floor one minute and fine the next, and since I can find no logical explanation for a badly bleeding wound which didn't exist, or for the stinky, black mist which rose out of you right after we prayed over you, I'm going to keep an open mind. Who is—was— Richard Pantino?"

Bart dropped his head and studied his feet. He looked at Ken.

"His family was my first big case after becoming sheriff. Pantino—or my hallucination of Pantino—rocketed me back in time.

"Richard called to report his wife, Dana, and children missing. I spent every day searching for clues to locate the family. Two weeks later, all three of them were found in shallow graves ten miles south of Ravens Cove. The children had been assaulted; the mother, too.

"Pantino hated the sight of me, and who could blame him? He tried to get me fired; when it didn't work, he took every opportunity to remind me of the deaths. A year later, Richard blew his head off with a sawed-off shot gun."

"We can't win them all, you know," Ken said, his tone empathetic not judgmental.

"I tell myself I'm not at fault. Never could convince myself, though. Anyway, the thing bit me; felt like a spider bite, but a hundred times more painful. Then I blacked out until I saw you three looking down on me."

Paul nodded in understanding.

Ken's eyes were wide as Frisbees, still wondering if his fellow officer had a mini breakdown.

Paul spoke. "We are in for a battle, gentlemen. Our town is under siege, Sheriff, but not by humans. This is spiritual warfare. I was wrong to doubt Josiah Williams; we need to go talk to him. He knows much about this thing. I believe God sent him here to help us."

"He's a suspect."

"Did he come out of his cell and murder these twins, all by his lonesome?" Ken asked.

"Not helping, Melbourne," Bart answered.

"Look, as crazy as it sounds, this spiritual warfare thing is beginning to have some credence. The facts aren't adding up. Unless we factor in—and I can't believe I'm saying this—the supernatural.

"All I witnessed with you tonight, not to mention the weird voice coming from the ravine, are giving this case a creepy, unearthly feel. Maybe in the light of day I'll think myself foolish. Standing here in the eerie silence, I'm leaning toward Pastor Paul's explanation."

"Ok. Let's say your theory is correct. What next?" Bart asked Ken.

"Haven't a clue," Ken answered.

"Maybe Josiah Williams has some answers," Paul said. He started down the trail and stopped. "Where's the light from?"

Ken and Bart turned toward Ravens Cove. Smoke drifted above the lights of the town.

"Something's on fire!" Bart said. He sprinted toward town while punching numbers on his cell phone to alert the volunteer fire chief.

CHAPTER 24

OUT OF THE ASHES

Paul's heart pounded in his chest when he realized the direction of the smoke and light.

"Please God, please. Not the church!" He broke into a full run. He reached the street where the small house of worship sat.

It *was* his church. It was burning. Worse, a mob stood in front of it cheering with each snap of a burned beam. Paul's heart broke. His resolve broke with it.

"Why, God, why?" he whispered, tears running down his face, "have I been so wrong in Your calling?"

The crowd pushed in on him.

He knew these people; they were parishioners of the Congregational Alliance, each and every one. The victorious gleam in their eyes said it all.

"No reason to stay now, is there *Pastor*?" Gary the librarian's assistant spat at him.

"We'd help you pack up the church, but there isn't much left. So should be easy for you and your wife to get out of here," Erwin yelled.

Bart assessed the crowd. He knew a mob mentality, and he knew Paul was in physical danger. The hatred in these people was alive. He put himself between Paul and the throng.

Ken came up and stood beside him, his gun drawn.

The crowd stopped moving forward.

Ken held out Bart's .357. "Forgot to give you this earlier. Kat thought you'd want to have it."

"Thanks." Bart holstered his weapon. He looked into the mob. "What is wrong with you people?" he yelled, "this man is a member of our town! He has been for months. What has he done to you?"

"He lies. All he preaches is guilt and fear!" Erwin screamed. "He's not welcome in this town!"

"Not your call, Erwin."

The horde pushed forward.

Bart and Ken held their ground.

A rock whistled past Ken's ear. Ken fired a shot into the air.

Bart stayed Ken's hand. "You people go home before something happens we all regret."

No one moved.

"Get out of here, or so help me, I will arrest each and every one of you right here, right now."

Grandma Bricken, Kat, and a few members of Paul's church stepped out of the shadows. They stood, unified, with Ken and Bart.

Paul prayed.

The members of his church joined him, holding hands, bowing heads.

A small dirt cloud rose up in front of the angry mob. It started twirling. As it did, a cold breeze began to blow.

The wind increased in strength until the throng could no longer hold their ground. Erwin fell backward. Gary followed. It was like life-size dominoes—one by one the mob toppled, falling into the person behind.

The dirt cloud vanished as fast as it appeared, and the wind stopped.

Confused and frightened, the crowd scattered.

"Does freak weather occur here often?" Ken spoke to Bart out of the side of his mouth.

"Nope."

"Sometimes, God answers prayer in a way no one can dispute. I believe it's called a miracle," Grandma said.

The fire department arrived, yanked the hoses from the truck and sprayed the structure, now completely engulfed in flames.

Tears again streamed down Paul's face. "Why, God, have You allowed the Evil Foe to destroy this place of worship? Why have You allowed the Congregational Alliance to prosper when they, indeed, serve Satan?"

Bart overheard Paul's plea. Sadness, then anger, gripped his heart. He placed a hand on Paul's shoulder. "Until the fire is out and we can assess the damage, there is nothing you can do. Why don't you come with us?"

Paul lifted his red, tear-stained eyes to Bart's clear, angry ones and nodded.

He, Ken, and Bart turned from the wreckage of Paul's treasured little church.

Walking toward Main and past his church goers, Paul overheard them discussing where to hold their next service and how to recover from the loss.

God's promise to make bad work for the good of His beloved children hit Paul like the proverbial brick. The fire and frightening mob emboldened his small congregation, bringing them even closer together. His spirit lifted. Paul fell to his knees and called out to the church members. "Come. Join me in prayer."

The small group gathered around Paul, then knelt.

"Dear God, You have brought this church family together in only a way You can. Please grant us the grace and wisdom to forgive these people, dear Lord, and we ask You forgive them, too. In Jesus's mighty name. Amen."

"Amen." The little gathering echoed.

Paul stood. He strode over to Ken and Bart.

"It's time to bring this battle to our enemy. He's messing with the wrong church."

"He's messing with the wrong town!" Bart answered.

"Then let's go get some well-needed, even if they aren't believable, answers," Ken said.

CHAPTER 25

LEGEND OR TRUTH

Bart grabbed the keys from his desk drawer and walked down the narrow hall to the cell.

Josiah stood at the barred door, waiting expectantly.

Bart motioned Josiah away from the door and unlocked it. He turned and headed back to the main room of the office.

Josiah followed.

"Mr. Williams, I need you to tell us what you know about the chaos erupting in Ravens Cove."

"I believe you know the answer. Your real question is: How do we stop it?"

"Back to the confounded legend, isit?"

"The truth is the truth. In order to fight this thing, though, we must first get more information from Alese Bricken."

Bart's brow furrowed. "Grandma Bricken? How do you know her?"

"I have not met her. I was told about her—in a dream. She holds the key to victory."

"Really?" Ken said.

"Yes."

Well, we don't have time to debate this one. Last I saw her she was praying with Pastor here," Bart pointed his thumb toward Paul Lucas, "and other churchgoers."

"Then we go there." Josiah Williams grabbed his hat, plopping it atop his head.

Kat saw them coming before Grandma did. "Now what?"

Grandma put her hand on Kat's upper arm. "I believe they are here for me, Katrina."

She stiffened and took in a deep breath. She did not know the man beside Pastor Paul, but she saw him in a dream. She passed the vision off as an old woman's fancy and forgot about it—until now.

She released Kat's arm and stepped forward to greet them. "Why don't we go to my house, and I'll make some tea?"

Kat stared at her grandmother in shock and disapproval when Alese linked her arm through Josiah's as if she'd known him all her life.

Alese Bricken motioned for the others and Kat to follow.

"There's a lot I need to tell you, Josiah Williams," Grandma Bricken said, smiling into his eyes.

Josiah patted her hand. "Indeed there is, Ms. Alese; indeed there is." "Curiouser and curiouser," Kat said to Bart as they followed the duo up Main, left on Willow and right on Wild Rose to Grandma's immaculate cottage.

After she finished pouring tea in her best company cups, Grandma Bricken set the canary yellow and cream-colored teapot in the middle of her large round table.

"I believe you know the story?" she spoke to Josiah alone.

"Yes, ma'am."

"Well, the part of the story kept secret in my family for as long as it has been passed down, is the way to stop this thing and send it back to Hell where it belongs."

Kat's eyes opened in surprise. Hell was another word, no matter the context, not used in Grandma's presence. Even when trying to discuss *Dante's Inferno*, Grandma would not allow her granddaughter to use the word. *Made for a more difficult than normal discussion.*

Grandma patted Kat's hand, knowing she shocked her granddaughter. "I'm not always as prim and proper as I seem, Katrina."

"Why kept secret?" Josiah asked.

"In the wrong hands, the way to destroy this thing could be used to keep it here."

"I see."

"The demon has a pet, for lack of a better term. It is his lure, and it is dangerous. Looking into its pulsing lights is hypnotic. Once spellbound, it wounds the unsuspecting victim and takes possession of its prey.

"This pet must be taken from Iconoclast. If they are separated, Iconoclast's power diminishes. More importantly, if this thing is taken from Iconoclast, he loses his reign over all the land under his dominion since the fall of man.

"If he holds onto it, then he will obtain his fifth victim, and he will destroy this town and anything living in or around it. This is bad enough. But, if he succeeds here, then he will be powerful enough to do this all over the world, wherever he has dominion."

"And how are we supposed to get this pet?" Bart asked.

Grandma Bricken shook her head. "The legend doesn't say. But I'm praying God makes the way."

"In Jesus' name!" Paul answered.

"I am more troubled by the final warning in the legend," Grandma Bricken added.

"Things can get worse?" Kat asked.

"Yes. The tale says one destined to be God Almighty's child must be lured by the pet to be the fifth victim. It *must* be a soul snatched from the very hand of God."

"I don't know how this thing could ever get a fifth victim, then. God's people are never taken from God's hand," Paul said.

"I know, Pastor. Yet, Iconoclast must believe there is a way. Or he wouldn't keep trying."

"Hopefully, Iconoclast's arrogance will be his downfall," Josiah said.

"I do pray you are right, Mr. Williams," Grandma Bricken answered.

"To continue, this pet's attachment to Iconoclast is why he is allowed to continue to reside on this earth, instead of the abyss where he belongs.

"Most concerning, though, is Iconoclast has never taken four victims before. This is the closest he has ever gotten, at least from all the history handed down."

This peculiar posse, brought together by the events of the last twenty- four hours, sat in silence. The weight of her words lay heavy on each of their hearts.

Kat broke the silence. "When I brought up the legend to you Bart two days ago, I didn't know what I was saying."

"I know," Bart answered.

"If you had told me when I got here I would be in a battle with a nightmare, I would have left and never returned," Ken said.

"You can still leave, FBI," Kat answered.

Ken's eyes locked on Kat's. "I have never run from a fight with a bad guy. I'm not starting now."

"Even when the bad guy isn't flesh and blood?" Josiah asked.

"Even then."

"Neither have I," Bart said.

"Then we're agreed," Grandma Bricken said. "Let's take this battle to the enemy. And take it to him where he lives."

CHAPTER 26

A WOMAN SCORNED

Reverend Plotno stood outside his beloved domain, smiling with satisfaction while he watched the firelight illuminating the dark sky. To him, the smoke smelled like a pleasant cologne. His smile widened. "Goodbye to you Paul Lucas, and to your insignificant church! Goodbye."

He clapped as if applauding an outstanding performance before turning and marching into the Congregational Alliance to light incense and praise the guardians for his victory.

His obligatory thanks given, the Right Reverend Plotno stood once again on the steps of his small kingdom, overlooking the destruction of Paul Lucas's church. The odor of burnt wood drifted to his nostrils. He sighed in satisfaction.

So close behind him it might as well have been one with the Reverend, stood Atramentous, who grew even darker and stronger with the destruction of the tiny house of worship. He, too, smiled.

Anita jogged up the steps, breathless from the excitement of the night's events. "Isn't it wonderful?" she whispered, while sliding her hand into Plotno's, giving it a slight squeeze.

"It is indeed. I haven't been this happy since . . ." he furrowed his brow, then held up an index finger, "since before Paul Lucas invaded our town."

Anita put her free hand in her coat pocket feeling for the present prepared for Plotno. He coveted a good cigar. And Anita knew the one he favored. She bought it for him while in Anchorage a few months back— a gift of her heart, she told herself. At the time, Anita didn't know it would turn out to be a gift of *his* heart as soon as he smoked the love-potion laced cigar. Her spell excited her more because she knew he thought her a dolt. He believed he controlled her. For a while he did. A memory she detested.

Tonight, my love, the tables will be turned.

Anita disobeyed his command to go to the small, awful church and spy on the small, awful congregation. She went to her basement. Rebellion and secrecy were an intoxicating elixir. When practicing the black arts, the intoxication became so intense she could only equate it to having finally made love to a long-forbidden beau.

She first considered soaking the cigar in the potion but thought better of it. It would darken the tobacco leaves, and he might become suspicious. Anita rifled through her medicine cabinet and uncovered an ancient syringe. She injected the concoction into the center of the tightly rolled leaves. She watched with deep satisfaction as the potion disappeared into the tobacco, hidden just as it should be.

"Reverend, this is a present I have kept for you for such a special occasion as this."

Plotno took his eyes off the orange glow and the black smoke billowing up as the water put out the fire. He looked at the offering from Anita.

A broader smile crossed his face as he thought of the anger this would cause his wife, Ransom.

"You are a treasure! You understand our core ideology: what feels good is good. That wife of mine has never understood me like you do! She still worries about my health of all things! So short-sighted. But you understand the need for pleasure."

"I try," Anita whispered.

"You succeed." Plotno took the cigar, searching his pants pocket for a lighter.

"Here you go." Anita produced one.

The lighter glinted gold and black in his hand. His initials were carved into it, the black absorbing light.

"You thought of everything," he said as he flicked the lighter open, puffed the cigar until the tip glowed red and took a deep inhale. He exhaled and looked down at Anita.

"What a wonderful end to a wonderful day."

Profligacy went to work, whispering to his mind, "She is the loveliest thing you have ever seen, Plotno. Forget your wife. This one knows what you love, and she loves what you do. Feel the craving for her growing in your gut. She is your obsession! You must have her."

Plotno grabbed Anita around the waist. "I want you, and you know it. I can't wait any longer."

Anita smiled, took Plotno's hand and led him into the Congregational Alliance. "I know just the place. It will be delicious!"

The door closed, and Atramentous settled in to watch.

Venenose flew up beside Profligacy. "Good work."

"As always," Profligacy answered.

Venenose sneered in satisfaction. "All to be done now is alert the wife."

"Said. And done." Profligacy called to the demon Parlous, stationed at Plotno's residence.

"Now we wait," Venenose said.

"Why do I feel like I must go to the Congregational Alliance?" Mrs. Plotno asked herself. She fought the urge. "Not where I want to be. I despise the place."

She shook her head to try and clear the urgent need to go. "It's not because I don't love and take pride in Martin's stature in the community. But I have better things to do with my time than sit there and listen to him expound on feeling good and watching those Congregational Alliance groupies fall all over him. I get enough of his preaching at home.

"I'll bake a cake. That always gets my mind off something." Ransom headed for the kitchen.

Grab a knife. Something is wrong. Martin's in danger! said the voice of Parlous in her head.

Terror gripped Ransom Plotno's stomach. "Martin's in trouble!"

She yanked open the knife drawer and bolted to the living room. She grabbed her purse and threw on a coat.

Ransom dashed up the street, butcher knife in hand, toward the church to save her Martin.

Plotno and Anita were entwined in front of the Congregational Alliance's shiny, ornate altar.

"Now isn't this the best place to make our love commitment?" Anita whispered in his ear, feeling his heart racing against hers.

"Mmm."

Plotno and Anita were so engrossed in each other they didn't hear the door of the church open. In his haste, the Right Reverend neglected to lock it.

Ransom Plotno stopped midstride, grabbing the church door before it slammed. It took her a minute to believe what she saw. Truth flooded her. Rage filled her heart and mind and propelled her forward.

The butcher knife flashed when she pointed it at her target. She did not see people as she ran toward the objects of her rage—only the horror of being deceived and humiliated for so long.

The first blow felt great; blood spurted from Martin's neck. He fell atop Anita.

Anita screamed as she watched Martin's blood fly in the air from the knife.

Ransom raised the blade over the helpless Anita.

Anita watched the knife's rapid descent toward her right eye. She stopped screaming.

Martin fought a little longer. But in the end, he too lost the battle against the devoted wife turned assailant.

Ransom Plotno stared down at the bloody heaps on the floor and commented, "Looks like a bad load of laundry."

She raised her voice until it echoed off the stone walls. "That's exactly what you are, Martin Plotno, a bad load of laundry! Farewell and good riddance!"

Ransom walked calmly down the aisle to the door, then turned back. "Knifing you felt great, Martin, just like you always preached. Sorry I didn't listen to you sooner!" Holding the knife high, she broke out in wild laughter at her own joke and burst through the doors of the Congregational Alliance church.

Miggie blocked the staircase to the street.

Oblivious to the ghastly site of Miggie Salisto, she grinned at him.

Miggie smiled back, vacant sockets squishing the purple and black mixture from his eyes. "Well done, Ransom Plotno. You sure took your time giving the no-good jerk what he deserved!"

Ransom lowered the knife to her side. "You're sure right!"

"There are more who should meet the same fate tonight, don't you think?"

Ransom nodded. "I can come up with several members of this pack I'd like to see bleeding to death and hear screaming in terror—several women come to mind," she mumbled, running a finger along the blade's edge.

"Yes, many of them need to meet my new friend," she said, unaware the blade cut deep into her thumb causing the flesh to lay open and bleed freely.

"First, you need to meet my friend. He is most anxious to know you."

Ransom tensed and turned her dead eyes to Miggie's vacant ones.

"It's okay. He's your pal, too. In fact, he's the one who sent one of his soldiers to tell you about this tryst so you could set things right once and for all."

Ransom stood, torn between finishing her blood bath and going to see this supposed ally.

"He is very powerful. He can help you destroy the others. You don't have to do everything alone anymore."

"Oh, I like that idea! Take me to him!"

Jo, returning from the tragic fire at the small church she loved, saw a sight horrifying her beyond words.

"God, help us." She ducked beside the Congregational Alliance's wall and peeked around the corner.

Ransom Plotno stood under a streetlight in front of the church. Maroon stripes covered her arms and the front of her legs. Small, red droplets adorned the front of her clothes and streaked her dark cherry Kool-Aid colored hair like macabre highlights.

Looks like a bad paint job, Jo thought.

A large butcher knife, shining with the same blood-red liquid, hung at Ransom's side.

Ransom carried on an animated, one-sided conversation. She sauntered out from under the light, still talking to her unseen companion.

When Jo could see her no longer, she came out of hiding and made her way to the bottom of the church stairs.

"It's blood, sure as life." She lifted her eyes and saw footprints of scarlet leading from the church to the streetlight. She darted for the sheriff's office.

Atramentous smiled as he watched Jo skittering like a scared rabbit toward her destination.

"Run, little rat, run. The Sheriff will do you no good. The plan is coming together nicely. I can already taste the feast being prepared for me and all of Iconoclast's soldiers."

He pulled away from the church door, no longer needing to guard it and slithered up beside Ransom, flanking her on the left, Miggie still on her right.

Miggie nodded to Atramentous. "This is Atramentous, Ransom. One of your many new friends."

"Hello," Ransom said.

"Good evening, madame. I am pleased to meet you," Atramentous answered.

Atramentous studied the blood-covered late Reverend's wife. "More pleased than you can ever know."

Atramentous narrowed his eyes and thought, *You have no idea what horrors await you. But you are a pivotal player in Iconoclast's plan. And I am going to get you safely to the ravine—and your eventual destruction.*

CHAPTER 27

SAFETY IN NUMBERS

An empty and dark sheriff's office greeted Jo. She ran to Bart's home. No luck there, either. She headed back to the office, rounded a corner and bulldozed Caroline, knocking them both to the ground. "Oomph!" Caroline's library books flew through the air like dancing ballerinas.

"Oh! Caroline! I'm so sorry!" Jo kneeled to gather the novels scattered around them.

"What's the hurry?"

"Have you seen the Sheriff?"

"No, maybe he's at home."

Jo shook her head while trying to catch her breath.

"Sit down, you look terrible." Caroline motioned to the bench in front of the shop.

Jo plopped down.

"What's happening?"

"Murder!" Jo wheezed while gasping for air.

"What are you talking about?"

"Ransom Plotno's murdered someone!"

"Omigosh! You must be mistaken, Jo. Ransom Plotno is the mousiest woman on Earth. She's scared of her own shadow!" *I never did understand how she caught such a wonderful, handsome man as the Reverend*, Caroline thought.

"It was Ransom! I saw her! Big as life!"

Caroline resisted the urge to cover hear ears from Jo's deafening trill.

"And she was bat-crazy! She looked like someone out of *The Texas Chainsaw Massacre*—standing in front of the CA church—blood from head to toe. I thought it was paint at first, then I saw the butcher knife dangling from her hand. I need to find the Sheriff!"

"Well, I still can't believe it was Ransom, Jo, she's way too mild." Caroline unlocked the door to her salon, Jo trailing behind.

Caroline retrieved her cellphone and punched in a number.

"Who are you calling?"

"Kat Tovslosky. If anyone knows where Bart is, she will."

The phone rang and rang.

Caroline hung up and thought. She punched in another number.

Grandma Bricken willed herself to ignore the phone. The events of the last few days created a need to stay focused on the small group conversation.

The phone continued ringing.

"Oh, for heaven's sake." She pushed herself back from the table and walked from the room.

Bart watched her leave, then said, "We have no clue who this fifth victim is to be. And I don't want another death on my hands. I've seen enough death to last me a lifetime. Starting a lumberyard is sounding better all the time."

"Bart. BART!"

"What?" Bart yelled.

"Caroline's on the phone. Sounds urgent."

"Unless there's been another murder, or another fire for that matter, tell her I'll call her back. This town! Jaywalking is urgent," Bart said to the group.

"He'll call you back."

"Grandma! Get Bart on the phone! Jo is with me, says there's been another murder! This time at the Congregational Alliance."

Bart watched the doorway, waiting for his great-aunt to return.

Grandma Bricken held the phone for the Sheriff. "Another killing."

Bart jumped up and grabbed the receiver.

Grandma's face was ash grey. She walked back to the table and fell into her chair. "There's been another murder."

Kat and Ken simultaneously exclaimed, "What!"

Bart poked his head in the door to the kitchen. "Iconoclast seems to have claimed his last victim. I need to get to the Congregational Alliance." He grabbed his hat from the peg at Grandma's door.

"Not the one, Sheriff. Otherwise, we wouldn't be sitting at this table right now. We'd be fighting for our lives," Josiah answered.

"No matter if it is the fifth or not there's another body, and I gotta go."

Grandma rose and headed to the hallway.

So did the rest of the group.

"We're all coming with you," Kat said.

"No, you're not."

"Listen, Cousin. You ended up in a puddle on the floor tonight and almost blew your brains out. Mom always said, 'safety in numbers.' We're going with you."

"Suit yourself." Bart hurried out the door.

The Sheriff and his impromptu deputies walked to the Congregational Alliance. It loomed above Main Street—tomb silent.

At the foot of the steps, Bart motioned for all to stop. "Stay. Except you, Melbourne."

Bart and Ken walked to the top of the stairs.

Ken drew his gun. "Ready?"

"Yep."

They moved quickly into the building.

Bart pointed to Ken to take the right.

Bart took the left. "Clear on this side."

Gun held chest level, Ken crept up the right side of the sanctuary. He lowered the gun. "Clear."

They met at the altar. The scantily dressed bodies of Martin Plotno and Anita Conner lay exposed for all to see.

Ken let out a low whistle. "The saints preserve us."

Bart checked for a pulse on both and shook his head at Ken. He released his phone from its case and called Doc Billings.

"On my way."

"Whoever is responsible for this massacre sure hated the reverend, not to mention the librarian."

"Oh, yeah," Ken agreed. "The carnage is overkill. Look at the way Anita's eyes have been gouged out, and the late reverend's back and neck look like hamburger."

"If Ransom did find out about this affair, it's conceivable she snapped," Bart answered.

"Yep. We best find her—and fast."

"We go together. I don't want either of us looking for a crazed killer without backup."

"Agreed."

Bart jogged across the street to Kat, Grandma Bricken, Pastor Lucas, and Josiah. He looked around. "Where's Wendy? I thought she'd have caught wind of this by now."

"You know Wendy. The only thing to trump her love of good drama, is her loyalty to her sister. Seems Mandy is missing—again. She left for Anchorage and told me to call her with any updates."

"Well, it's best. One less person to fear for."

Kat nodded. "Understand."

"Three things: First, it's a horrible scene. Anita Conner and Reverend Plotno are dead."

"Both of them?" Paul asked.

Bart held up a hand. "Yes. No time for questions. Second, Kat wait for Doc Billings to come and take care of the bodies. Then, find Jo and Caroline, tell them to go to Caroline's. We'll be there as soon as we can."

"Sure thing." Kat watched Bart run back to the church.

Doc Billings' unmistakable Audi slid up to the curb.

"Evening," he said.

Kat pointed. "In the church, Doc."

Billings grabbed his bag from the passenger's seat, jogged up the steps and into the church.

"Lord, show us what to do," Paul began. "You, O God, are sovereign, even when the world or the situation shouts to us that You are not. Please help us to know what we are to do, O God. We cannot stop or defeat what is happening in our beloved town but, God, You can. Please grant us strength."

When Grandma and Josiah bowed their heads in agreement, Kat followed suit.

"In Jesus's name. Amen."

The funeral home's black hearse pulled up fifteen minutes later.

"This is going to be a long night," Kat said.

"How could this happen?" Grandma asked.

Josiah answered, "Lust and jealousy are involved."

He turned and looked down the street toward the small church standing no longer. He longed to go there. To get away from the horror he felt building, a tangible evil working up for the kill, so close he could almost touch it.

CHAPTER 28

JO'S STRANGE STORY

"I can't believe a person covered in blood can just disappear," Bart said.

"We've looked at her house, and her friends' homes. She's nowhere to be found," Ken answered.

"Let's get to Caroline and Cassie's house, and then go back out again." Ken nodded.

Caroline opened the door. "Cassie is sleeping. So, please be as quiet as you can."

"Of course," Bart answered.

Bart and Ken listened, working to believe Jo's strange story.

"That's some story, Jo," Bart said.

"You know I'm down-to-earth, Bart. I don't believe in this supernatural mumbo jumbo. But the way Ransom looked . . . she was a whole different person. A really creepy person."

A knock interrupted the questioning. Caroline ushered Kat, Grandma Bricken, Paul and Josiah into the room.

Bart continued, "You sure it was Ransom?"

"Sure as I'm looking at you Bart! Her hair color alone gave her away—You know, the cherry Kool-Aid color?"

"Yeah. It's definitely unique."

"And she carried on an intense conversation with no one . . . at least no one I could see."

"Hmmm." Bart knew Jo pooh-poohed anything which could not be seen, felt, touched, smelled, or tasted. The supernatural nonsense being just that—nonsense. He sighed. Tonight, her concrete world shattered.

Caroline stood statue-still nodding her head up and down like a bobblehead.

"I've never seen Jo this upset since . . ." Grandma said.

"Since when?" Josiah asked.

"Since her husband left." Grandma shook her head. "Not relevant now."

"What should we do?" Pastor Lucas asked Grandma.

"Right now? We wait."

"One more thing, Sheriff. I think I know where Mrs. Plotno went," Jo said.

"Where?"

"She headed up Main and into the dark—in a hurry, like on a mission. If I were a swearing woman, I'd swear she headed to Ravens Ravine."

"The only place not checked," Bart murmured to Ken. "With all that's happened, I didn't think she'd be crazy enough to go up there. Jo, stay here with Caroline—at least until it gets light. Both of you try to get some rest."

Ken and Bart started up Main, the group falling in a few steps behind.

Bart turned. "Not you. This is way too dangerous."

"This is too dangerous for us *not* to join you," Josiah answered.

The group turned eyes on Bart and Ken.

"Legend or not, in good conscience, I cannot let you come along. How am I going to know I'm doing my job, when the two most important women in my life," Bart looked from Kat to Grandma Bricken, "would be heading right into the path of possible life-ending danger?"

"And how, Bartholomew, could I live with myself if I allowed my most beloved great-nephew to walk into definite spiritual death?"

A death scream ruptured the night's silence. It came from the direction of the ravine.

"That was no animal," Kat said.

Grandma's head shot up to Bart. She stared into his eyes. "We *will* be accompanying you tonight, Bartholomew Anderson!" She clutched her cane and started for the ravine.

CHAPTER 29

GUARDING THE RAVINE

Ransom Plotno sat cross-legged, facing town, back to the ravine path, just as instructed.

"Wait here," Atramentous told her. "My commander will meet you in due time. First, though, you are to guard the path for me and Miggie."

"Okay."

"Our enemies are coming, and they mean you harm. Prepare to fight. It is the only way you will survive."

Ransom held the knife, pointed skyward, both hands clutching the handle.

Miggie and Atramentous left to consult with Iconoclast.

"This is our chance," Martin said to Anita.

"Are you crazy? We will be tortured."

"The demons lied to us! They promised we'd take part in their banquet of destruction, and instead they destroyed us. They allowed this horrible woman," he pointed at his former wife with the stub of the finger he'd lost in the vain attempt to defend himself, "to destroy us. It's our turn."

As in life, Anita agreed.

They materialized.

"Ransom!" A macabre duet commanded her to look up.

Ransom's eyes widened. Her recently deceased husband and his latest tryst stood before her. The latter, covered with blood, focused on her through empty eye sockets.

Ransom's body quaked, forcing her to drop the knife.

"I am here to take you to Hell where you belong," Plotno said. He lunged forward.

"Oh, you will taste good!" Anita giggled and grabbed Ransom's wrists, holding her in a vice grip.

Ransom yowled in agony when Plotno and Anita latched onto her face and sucked. Skin unwrapped from her skull in lines like they were peeling an apple.

Iconoclast's head snapped back from the celebratory huddle with his minions. "Go!" He commanded Atramentous and Miggie.

They darted up the ravine.

Ransom Plotno lay in a heap. Her skinless face, deep maroon fluid seeping from the bare muscle and bone, greeted them.

"You fools!" Atramentous shouted. "You should have left well enough alone. Iconoclast will see you, *now*!"

Miggie grabbed Anita.

Atramentous looped around Plotno.

Together they dragged the pair into the pit.

Iconoclast dined on their souls—jagged, sharp teeth cutting their spirits apart piece by piece.

Iconoclast's minions shook. The endless screams reminded them of their own fate of endless torture in the abyss if they disobeyed the Commander.

CHAPTER 30

ANOTHER LOST SOUL

Ken jogged past Bart and arrived at the ravine first. He surveyed the scene. There lay a battered corpse, eyes wide and blank, face frozen in a scream. Steam rose from the skinless red mass which served as muscle and tendon and human being just moments before.

Bart joined Ken. "I believe we are looking at Ransom Plotno, the good Reverend's wife."

Ken gave him a questioning look.

"Hair color. The cherry Kool-Aid tint is unmistakable."

Ken nodded. "Right! Jo mentioned it. Definitely not a color one sees every day."

"She's not in the same position as the others," Bart noted.

Ransom lay several feet from the ravine pathway, sprawled on her back, dead eyes looking into the starless night sky.

"She doesn't smell like the others, either."

Ken stooped down, looking at, but not touching, the large blade at the corpse's side.

"Mrs. Plotno left-handed?" Ken asked.

"Not sure."

"There's a mean-looking butcher knife, coated in dried blood, beside her left hand."

Bart walked to Ken and shone the flashlight on the corpse. "A lot of good it did her. Why the hell didn't she use it to protect herself?"

"Bartholomew Andersen! Watch your language."

Bart pulled himself to his full height, blocking Grandma Bricken's view. "You need to go home now. This is no place for you."

"Really? And at home is the place to be? Waiting to be the next victim of this evil?" She pushed firmly on Bart's chest until he acquiesced and let her by.

Grandma's hand flew to her mouth to stifle an involuntary scream. Tears filled her eyes. "How horrible!"

"I told you to leave."

Grandma Bricken turned wet piercing-green eyes to Bart. "I'm not scared of seeing the dead, Bartholomew, I've seen much in my time. But I cry for the souls lost to God. Those losses are the true horror!"

Bart shook his head. "Ok, Gram."

Josiah walked up to the corpse. "This is not the work of Iconoclast," he said. "It is the work of evil but not of Iconoclast."

"How do you know, Mr. Williams?" Paul asked.

"I don't know it. I am surmising it. There is no smell. There is no purple and black liquid oozing from her eyes. Furthermore, this woman just murdered her husband and his lover. Why would she come up here instead of running for the hills, unless called here to be a part of Iconoclast's plan? If Iconoclast didn't take her, then she did not fulfill her part yet."

"Now what?"

"We wait; and we pray. The fifth victim will come. And we must stop him—or her—from going into the ravine."

The group bent their heads.

"Father in Heaven," Paul said. "We are almost in the Lion's den. We are afraid, and we are confused. Please send Your holy angels to fight with us. Please guide us; please help and protect us. In Jesus's mighty name."

Iconoclast's razor-toothed mouth widened into a horrible grin. "The fifth one is here!"

"Where?" Gambogian asked.

"At the top of the ravine, you fool."

"How do we get this one here?"

"We set a trap."

Iconoclast looked at the ink-black arrowhead in his clawed hand. "Pet, lure the one into my lair. But do not cut the body; do not touch the heart. If you do, I will destroy you! Do you understand?"

"Yes," Pet answered.

"This one is the key to opening the abyss and releasing more of Lucifer's angels. Earth's destruction will begin here in this insignificant town, and grow. Now go!" Iconoclast threw Pet to the top of the ravine.

"*Pet* do this; *Pet* do that! And just how am I supposed to entrap without possessing her?" Pet seethed, hatred coursing through his arrowhead shape, sending black tendrils out along the trail.

"How I long to come to my full height and be no one's servant. Iconoclast's captains have sniggered at me for centuries. Not for much longer!

"I'll show them! I may be small, but I'm as mean as any of them. I'll get this chosen one. And Lucifer will reward me with my own army! Then, I'll exact my revenge on all of them—Iconoclast first."

Pet searched the night for his prey. "There you are! Come to me—now!"

CHAPTER 31

THE TRAP

Kat opened her eyes and caught a glint of something at the top of the path. *Maybe it's evidence and would help reveal the killer's identity.*

She snuck away from the group. She knelt and admired a glowing purple and black arrowhead. The glimmering colors enraptured her.

"How do you make the colors so beautiful?" she murmured.

The speed of the changing lights quickened in response to her question. And a soft, melancholy tune emanated from the little treasure.

Kat smiled. "How pretty you are!"

Something niggled in the back of Kat's mind, something trying to remind her of danger.

The rock's enchanting hum clouded her thoughts. The fear of danger melted in the beautiful, sad tune. The multicolored hues quivered to its beat.

The hag tree rustled. Kat looked up, attention diverted from the beautiful colors and music. The tree swayed, invisible leaves tinkling in rhythm with the melody from the arrowhead.

Kat glanced at the downward path. She hesitated. *Not a good idea to go down there alone.*

She peered further into the murky darkness. More hag trees flanked the narrow walkway, each an exact replica of the one at the entrance. "They're shining!"

The cloned hag trees sparkled and swayed in time with the music. They created glittering specks of purple and yellow.

She stood, entranced by the strange and wondrous sights. *They look so beautiful and yet so ugly.*

She took a step forward to get a closer look.

The rustling grew louder.

Pet, who longed to cut her and take her, instead throbbed a calming beat in her hand.

The throb sent vibrations up Kat's arms and down her legs. She could *feel* the tune as well as hear it. Kat swayed, then danced to the music.

She looked back. The others were still deep in prayer, oblivious to this amazing phenomenon. She returned her focus to the ravine opening. The hag trees illuminated a once invisible doorway. Yellow strings dripped down its sides, reminding her of icicle lights decorating houses at Christmas.

I have to touch them! Kat took another step onto the ravine path.

Pet quickened the thrumming in approval, and his music grew louder.

Kat looked at the beautiful arrowhead.

An ochre aura surrounded her hand. Yet under Pet's spell, she observed it as a bright gold and emerald-green.

"I have never known anything so beautiful."

The trees and archway at the bottom of the ravine path alternated their hues to match the changing tints on Pet. The colors brightened each time Kat advanced on the trail.

The angel Uriel shouted "Josiah!" into his mind.

Josiah jumped to his feet and peered through the darkness. He saw nothing out of the ordinary. He searched again.

There. Josiah noticed a dim, mustard beam, laced with a sickening purple, glowing in the ravine. He watched the light grow in intensity.

The two pulsed and swirled, moving faster and faster, until they collided in a macabre swirl. The ochre and purple funnel filled the ravine and blocked the night sky.

"No, Lord, no!" he cried.

Bowed heads jerked up and turned to Josiah.

He pointed toward the pulsing funnel cloud above the ravine. "The fifth victim is close."

"Not possible! We would have heard or seen anyone coming," Ken answered.

Grandma Bricken looked to her right. Fear filled her heart. She grabbed Ken's hand and squeezed.

Ken followed her gaze. He saw the empty space where Kat once stood.

Alarm shot through the small group like a clap of thunder.

"Kat!" Bart yelled.

"Kat! Please answer!" Paul hollered.

"Oh, my Lord! Kat! Kat! Kat!" Grandma yelled.

Empowered by the Holy Spirit Grandma Bricken dropped her cane and ran like a young deer toward the ravine.

Josiah, Bart, Ken and Paul ran up beside her.

"Jesus, help us and Jesus, please help Kat!" Paul Lucas pleaded.

Halfway down the path, Kat hummed and picked imaginary leaves from the hag trees. A bright orb dropped in front of her.

"Ouch!" Kat shielded her eyes.

Raphael, the same angel who so long ago warned Sweeney of his imminent destruction in this very ravine, stood between Kat and the opening to the pit.

"Stop, Katrina Agnes Tovslosky!"

Kat came to a standstill. "I don't want to stop! See how pretty my treasure is?" she held Pet up to Raphael.

"It is not beautiful. What you mistake for beauty, Katrina, is a being bent on your eternal destruction."

Kat craned her neck to the right, then left. "Rats! I can't see around this THING surrounding you!"

She stomped her foot and tried again to peek around the wall of light. She let out a heavy sigh and sat down, confused.

Raphael waited. Unless this lost but beloved child of the Most High ordered him to leave, he would stay.

Kat looked up at the angel. "You are tall," she observed.

Raphael towered above the hag trees, which stood more than eight feet high.

"Really tall," she said.

Pet went silent, hiding from the warrior of God.

As Kat's confusion grew, he became bolder.

"Go away, Raphael!" Pet hummed loudly in hopes of breaking the being of light's tentative hold.

The angel scrutinized the purple and black arrowhead in Kat's hand. "Katrina, you should drop the stone. It has confused your thinking, your emotions."

Kat looked down at the small, beautiful jewel. She stroked its rough surface... then tightened her grip like a vise.

"No! I found it, it is mine!" She said, staring with defiance into the angel's eyes.

"It makes me feel better—you do not! In fact, now I feel sad. You are the bad one here, go away!"

Raphael looked upon Kat in sorrow.

"So be it." He shot up like a rising star in the darkness.

Kat stood. "What if he is right?"

"He isn't," a resonant, warm voice answered from inside the ravine. The archway glittered, and the hag trees swayed.

"No, he isn't right," Kat agreed.

Kat resumed singing the melancholy melody which served as her death march. She took another step forward.

CHAPTER 32

INTO THE RAVINE

Alese Bricken walked onto the ravine path.

"Whoa!" Kenneth grabbed her arm, just as she lost her footing.

"Thank you, young man."

The rest of the group stood in a semicircle around her. The smell of decaying corpses assaulted their senses.

Kenneth looked into the ravine and saw a black void.

Josiah looked into the ravine and saw a crystalline plume streaking toward the heavens. In the waning brilliance, Josiah was sure he saw the silhouette of a woman,

"She's down there!"

Bart stared at Josiah. "You're seeing things, old man. It's black as midnight down there."

Ken nodded agreement with Bart.

"I know what I saw!" Josiah shouted.

Alese laid a hand on Josiah's forearm. "I believe you."

"We must go, or she is lost!" Josiah said and headed to the ravine opening.

Alese released a determined breath and took a step forward.

Again, Ken grabbed her arm. "Too steep."

"I must go." She pulled her arm loose.

"Not by yourself." Ken offered the crook of his arm.

"Look at me, Kenneth Melbourne. Am I holding my cane? Do I look like I need your help to stand? No! I'm going after my niece!

"As for you, this is the greatest danger you have ever faced. Are you willing to lose your life to save Kat? Are you willing to lose your *soul*? Because that is what we are facing. Life and death. And eternity. So, are you?"

Ken never thought about dying. He liked living. In fact, he thrived on the thrill of each day. *So, am I willing to die tonight?* He looked into Alese's challenging eyes.

The answer surprised even him. *If Kat's in danger, yes, I'm going to save her or die trying. She's gotten under my skin in a way no woman ever has. She is a puzzle I want to solve. It makes no sense, but I could be—no, I am— in love with her.*

"I'm going with you."

"We're all going," Alese stated. "Remember, safety in numbers."

"We can't all go," Bart said. "The path is too small. And it is no place for you."

"I'm going, Bart. That's my Katrina, and I need to get to her."

Bart sighed. "Auntie, I would give you the world, but I want you to stay here." He lifted her arm, and placed it on Paul's.

"Don't let her go down there!" Bart instructed Paul.

"Go get your cousin!" Paul squeezed Alese's shoulder.

Bart pulled his flashlight from his belt. The shaft of light illuminated a few inches at a time. The darkness absorbed the rest.

He wiggled a thin, dead willow trunk free from beside the path to use as a walking stick.

Bart and Ken started down the path, single file, slipping on rocks, ripping clothing on trees and shrubs cloaked by the dark.

The humming ceased. The ravine fell dead silent.

"Kat," Bart yelled, "Kat, are you down there?"

Deep-socketed, hollow eyes stared out from behind the hag trees and brush on the left of the path.

Hundreds of eyes joined in and watched every move Bart and Ken made.

Ken looked back over his left shoulder. He could not see where the path began.

"I can't shake the feeling we are being watched."

"Me either. Hoping it's just nerves," Bart answered.

Heavy air filled the ravine. Only the men's labored breaths disturbed the eerie silence.

Alese watched Bart and Ken disappear into the darkness.

"I will not stand here and do nothing!"

Josiah squeezed her arm. He knew what awaited Ken and Bart. "We can pray. Be of good cheer, as the Lord says, and believe. He has overcome the world.'"

Alese nodded and knelt.

Josiah and Paul followed her lead.

Alese prayed. "We are but a small, spiritual army, Lord. But we are *Your* army. Please send Your mighty angels to help us in this battle. Make us as strong as any the earth has seen by fighting this battle for us. The world is one person away from being destroyed. PLEASE help us. In Jesus' name."

Kat stopped advancing to the archway and listened.

"Kat, where are you?" Ken yelled.

"KittyKat, answer me, please!" Bart hollered.

Kat opened her mouth to answer.

Pet hummed louder, to drown out the voices.

She swung away from the dark opening.

"No, turn back, you will find rest, once you go into the cavern. Go to your destiny!"

Kat hesitated, then turned back to the doorway.

CHAPTER 33

AGAINST ALL ODDS

Bart made slow progress, fighting back the overgrowth on the path. It returned as quickly as he knocked it down.

Richard Pantino materialized and grabbed for him. "You are a loser, will always be a loser," he chanted.

Bart barely managed to sidestep the fleshless fingers.

"You stupid fool! You're in my world now. I can and will take you!" Pantino shot forward.

The twins, ghosts of Jonathan and Joseph Northan, materialized between Ken and Bart.

"We love fresh meat!" they said. "You have to be better than those tiny ravens would have been." They moved in on Ken.

Ken willed his feet to move, to run. They didn't.

Lightning flashed before Ken and Bart.

Uriel appeared.

The twins and Pantino sizzled and evaporated into the path.

Bart and Ken fell to their knees, shaking.

"Bartholomew Nelson Anderson, Kenneth Charles Melbourne, do not be afraid. I am Uriel, an archangel of the Most High. You have mighty prayer warriors interceding for you against this immutable evil. Our Lord, Jesus Christ, has heard their prayers. He has sent me to aid you.

"The evil spirits here will trouble you no more. The evil in the ground will trouble you no more. I will open your eyes to the spirit world.

"But I cannot intervene with the one named Katrina Agnes Tovslosky. She has free will to make her choice. You are her hope. Go to her!"

The brilliance dimmed. The path lay bare of underbrush everywhere Uriel's fiery light touched.

Ken shook his head. "Bart?"

"Yeah, I saw it. You okay?"

"Yeah, physically, anyway."

A short laugh escaped Bart. "Ditto."

"Seems our little group's praying. I've never been one for talking to God, but I might start," Ken said.

An eerie song floated on the dead air toward Ken and Bart.

There's a summer place where it may rain or storm yet I'm safe and warm. . .

Ken stared at Bart.

"Yeah I heard it. It's Kat's voice. Almost didn't recognize it."

"Me neither. The tone is both airy and dead."

Bart pointed. "There she is!"

A spine-chilling Kat lookalike faced them, yellow glinting from her eyes. She talked to a pitch-black rock in her hand.

"Do you see what she's holding, Ken?"

Ken squinted in an effort to focus on the ink-black arrowhead. Purple tendrils snaked upward from the sharp rock. Long, misty fingers shot out from the semi-transparent chords and circled Kat's head like a dirty halo.

"It's got arms! It's holding her head! Kat!" Ken called.

"God help us!" Bart said. "Katrina! Drop the arrowhead! It's a demon. Drop it now!"

Kat tried in vain to look up from her newfound treasure. The spirit world enveloped her, breaking her will. The more she beheld this beautiful arrowhead, the more it drew her in.

"I feel so good; so relaxed. I never want to feel fear and anxiety again. Never. I don't want to go back," she said.

"You don't have to," Pet pulsed in reply.

"Kat." Ken this time.

Who was that? She felt a tingle of excitement but couldn't understand why. She lifted her eyes from the stone, saw nothing and returned her gaze to her new friend.

"What's your name?" she asked.

"Pet," it responded.

"Why does that sound so familiar? Have we met before?"

"Maybe in your dreams. I have been waiting for you a long, long time. But my master has been waiting for you even longer. We should get going. He is not a patient one."

"Okay."

Katrina Agnes Tovslosky, stop now!" Bart yelled.

"Kat, no!" Ken screamed.

Kat continued her journey down the path.

Josiah slipped away from Alese and Paul. "Your will, not mine, Lord," he said and grabbed hold of the underbrush beside the ravine path and descended, caution in every step.

He hadn't gone far before Miggie appeared before him.

"Leave now, old man, or I'll take you to Iconoclast. He'll eat you alive."

Fear grew inside Josiah, as he looked into death's—no, Hell's eyes. He shook himself. "Be gone, evil one. You have no power over me. I am the Lord's."

Angered, Miggie lunged forward, teeth bared.

Josiah stood his ground.

"The Lord Jesus Christ rebuke you!" Josiah yelled. He thrust his arms forward.

Miggie fell backward, mouth agape, fury on his eyeless, bloody face.

Josiah bowed his head. "Thank you for the victory, my Lord."

"Amen!" Alese and Paul answered.

Josiah turned and smiled. "So be it, we go as one!"

"So be it," they responded.

Bart and Ken stood helpless. Neither knew how to prevent the woman they both loved, in different ways, from heading through the ravine archway.

"How do we get her attention?"

"I wish I knew," Ken answered.

"God, you know I'm not a praying man. Not much of a believer, either. Tonight is changing me. If You will, please help us!" Bart said.

"Amen!" Ken responded.

"Kat!" Bart yelled again.

Kat felt a tug at her heart. She stopped short of the opening and looked back. *Who's calling my name? I know the voice; I miss the person. Who are you?*

An overwhelming sadness blanketed her heart. Tears welled in her eyes and streamed down her cheeks.

"Silly, no one else is here," Pet said. "No one loves you like I do. No one will love you like the Commander. Step in, Kat."

Josiah, Alese, and Paul reached Ken and Bart.

"Bart! Ken!" Paul called out.

They turned, losing focus on Kat.

When the group came together, an angel army appeared. Their blinding light shattered the darkness.

The brilliance forced the hag trees to shrink into the ravine walls.

Kat stood inches from the entrance to the cavern's opening.

"It's now or never!" Ken lunged forward.

Josiah jumped in front of Ken, with the agility of a man half his age and grabbed Kat's arm, pulling with all his might.

Ken gripped her other arm.

Kat's demon possessed supernatural strength kept her in place.

Josiah noticed her hand closed in a fist. "Katrina, open your hand!"

"No, it's mine!"

"Katrina dear, open your hand. Let me see what you have there." Alese cooed to the confused child before her.

"Where did she come from? For that matter, where did they all come from?" Bart whispered to Ken.

"Don't know."

Kat's soulless eyes sparked in response to her grandmother's voice.

Grandma cupped Kat's head in her hand and lifted it. She looked Kat in the eye. "I will not steal it or take it unless you allow me to; but let me see your new prized possession, my sweet one."

Kat blinked twice and squinted at the woman before her. Her grip loosened around the rock.

Gambogian materialized in front of the cave opening. He opened his leathery wings and flew at Alese Bricken. The *crack* shattered the ravine's silence.

"She is ours!" his razor-sharp claws snapped open and he lunged at Alese's neck.

"Surround Alese Bricken!" Uriel commanded his angel army.

The angel army rushed to Alese Bricken and created a wall of light around her.

Each angel pointed a fiery sword toward the starless night sky.

Gambogian floated to the ground and snapped his wings shut.

"You do not belong here!" he roared.

"We belong where the Almighty God sends us!" Uriel replied. He leveled his sword at Gambogian.

Gambogian extended his arm toward the sky. Crimson red sparks flew from his hand. An ebony sword materialized.

The deafening clang of ethereal swords filled the ravine.

Gambogian and Uriel shot up into the night sky, thunder and lightning danced above the group as the battle continued.

"You are scaring me!" Kat said. She stepped backward toward the arch.

Josiah yelled. "God, help us!"

"Our ways have failed, O God. You are our only hope," Paul said.

"Please, God, hear our prayer," Alese pleaded.

"Amen," Bart said.

A frigid gust of wind blew up from the ravine floor. A voice, more a growl, thundered, "Leave here! This is MY domain!"

"You'll have all of us and more if we do, Iconoclast," Josiah answered.

Atramentous materialized, wrapped clawed talons around Kat's neck and squeezed. "Leave or she dies now!"

Kat gasped for breath. Her hands flew to her neck, clawing at her assailant.

Pet fell from her hand, bounced and stopped short of the archway.

Paul picked up the sick tarry thing Kat guarded a short while ago. He pulled a handkerchief from his back pocket and wrapped it up.

Kat lost consciousness, limp in the clutches of the dark mist.

Atramentous was so intent on controlling Kat, he did not see Josiah step backward through the archway into the darkness.

Alese noticed and watched in horror as he disappeared.

"I have come to slay you, slayer of my family!" Josiah roared.

"I will deal with you later." Atramentous released Kat and flew into the blackness of the cave.

The laughter rose, then a growl.

"I will send you to the abyss!" Josiah threatened.

Only silence came from the hollow.

"What are we doing here?" Kat asked, rubbing her eyes like a small child waking from a nap.

Grandma grabbed Kat and pulled her close. "My baby, my baby."

Bart put his arms around both women and pulled them into a huge bear hug. He rested his chin on Kat's head and smiled.

Ken stood back. *I want to grab you, yell at you, then hold you forever.*

Paul, elated by the victory moments before, glared at the archway. "I don't hear Josiah; I don't see him."

Ken, Bart, and Alese turned to the cavernous hole.

Kat snuggled closer in her Grandmother's arms.

The earth groaned, and small rocks bounced to the ground.

"Now what?" Bart's eyes grew saucer-sized as the arch shook and collapsed. A mountainous rock, as tall as the ravine itself, took its place.

"Where's Josiah?" Kat asked.

Grandma lifted her head, pointing with her chin to the boulder.

Tears filled Kat's eyes. "Crazy old man," she whispered.

"Crazy, but oh so brave," Grandma answered.

Kat nodded, then looked at Ken. It was his voice that she heard above that beautiful music.

Ken smiled.

She smiled back, then put her head on Grandma's shoulder and sobbed.

EPILOGUE

THE LEGEND SLEEPS

The tired group started the long walk up the ravine path. The loss of their companion weighed heavy on their hearts. Even in sadness, none of them could deny the gratitude they felt for Josiah Williams.

"What do we do with this thing?" Paul unwrapped the handkerchief as he spoke.

A small pile of ash lay in the arrowhead's place. He looked up in astonishment.

Grandma smiled. "Burn the handkerchief, Pastor. I believe Pet is no more."

Ken wedged himself between Bart and Kat. "I need to talk to you, Kat."

Kat gave him a suspicious glance. In spite of her best efforts, her heart thumped a little faster, but she continued up the hill.

The small assembly reached the top of the ravine as day dawned. The old hag tree stood ugly as ever.

For the first time Grandma could remember, a small, brown sparrow perched on one of its misshapen branches singing its morning greeting. Grandma smiled and turned to watch the small group she loved so greatly.

Bart turned to Paul. "So, tell me about Jesus Christ, Pastor."

Paul clapped Bart on the back. "With pleasure, Bart, with pleasure."

Ken stopped, turned Kat to face him and held onto both her arms. Kat looked at him in surprise.

"I think I love you, Katrina Agnes Tovslosky."

189

Kat stood, unable to move, searching his face. Red crept up her neck. "Don't use my middle name."

"Got it."

"You better."

"Anyway, your grandmother asked me if I was willing to die for you before I went into the ravine. She seemed to know the answer, even before she asked it. And, you know, I kinda, sorta, decided I was..."

"Good to know, FBI." Kat punched him in the arm.

Grandma Bricken came alongside Kat. "Tell him you love him, too, Katrina. You know you do."

"Grandma!" Kat scolded.

"Well?"

Kat ignored the question. "I've seen things I don't understand and can't explain. I need to figure out what happened to me. I think Pastor Paul knows."

She looked at Grandma Bricken. "I sure liked the old man."

"I miss him, too. But he was a man of God and he is a man of God no matter what."

Kat nodded. If her grandmother said those words a couple of days ago, she would have rejected the statement as foolish. *Not now.*

Kat planted a swift peck on Grandma Bricken's cheek and rushed to the other side of Pastor Paul.

Ken snapped his cell phone shut, walked up beside Grandma Bricken and took her arm. "The chief okayed a few more days at the Cove, to wrap things up."

Ken focused on Kat in the distance. *It won't be easy to wrap up the case; but it'll be a piece of cake compared to getting Kat to finish our conversation.*

"Not to worry, Kenneth. She'll come back to you soon. And when she does, you better be ready to take her on, the cantankerous BC and all."

Grandma Bricken wrapped both her arms around his forearm. "Welcome to the family, Kenneth Melbourne. Welcome to Ravens Cove."

Ken stared down at her and grinned. "Welcome to Ravens Cove, indeed," he said, squeezed her hand and led her down the hill.

www.ingramcontent.com/pod-product-compliance
Lightning Source LLC
Chambersburg PA
CBHW051121260626
47170CB00005B/1605